THE SUN GODDESS

of Cargill's Castle

NEISHA NILSEN

Copyright © 2019 Neisha Nilsen

ISBN: 978-0-473-48048-6 (Softcover) 978-0-473-48049-3 (Epub)
978-0-473-48050-9 (Hardcover) 978-0-473-48051-6 (Kindle) 978-0-
473-48052-3 (ibook)

This is a work of fiction. Names, characters, places, and incidents
are a product of the author's imagination. Locales and public names
are sometimes used for atmospheric purposes. Any resemblance to
actual people, living or dead, or businesses, companies, events,
institutions, or locales is completely coincidental.

DEDICATION

I wrote this story for my beautiful daughter Brooke. I wanted to write something she could read as a young teenager, and here it is - my YA book "The Sun Goddess of Cargill's Castle."

ACKNOWLEDGMENTS

Another book done, go me! The Sun Goddess of Cargill's Castle was written for and totally inspired by my daughter Brooke. My previous books weren't something my teenager would be interested in and I wanted her to read something that I had written... so the story of Brigid began. A big clap for Robyn Flynn, Jamie Flynn and my awesome husband Nick Nilsen for reading my drafts and giving me advice to make this story better. I'd also like to thank my friends and family who I force to read my books, thanks for persevering with my craziness.

I write because I have a story in my head and it needs to come out. Once it takes root, it must go on paper or it will drive me insane.

CHAPTER 1

I followed the music as it enticed me closer towards its melody like the Pied Piper. I floated towards the sound, up some wide stairs and stopped in front of a pair of elaborately decorated wooden doors. Two butlers dressed in their black and white finery opened the doors for me and the music boomed out as it escaped its confines of the ballroom. It was magical. Women danced beautifully in brightly coloured dresses, their tiny waists pinched in with corsets, their hair piled high on their perfect heads, with small stray strands tickling their cheeks. Men were dressed in their finest black suits matched with their shiny black shoes. The men and women danced closely together in pairs and they looked spectacular. I looked up at the magnificent chandelier hanging from the ceiling and marveled at how the reflecting candlelight flickered and danced over the walls. I could feel the joy, feel the emotions of these people. I put my head back and laughed as I spun with my arms out wide. I knew this was a dream and what a great dream it was. I watched as a young brown haired girl around the age of ten, pull her father onto the dance floor. His smile touched my insides as he lifted his daughter and balanced her little feet on top of his perfectly black shiny shoes. Her squeal filled the room as they twirled around the dancefloor with her ringlets swinging wildly in the air behind her. The painted walls came alive with the shadows of the dancers, the fire and the candles. What a magical place, I didn't want to leave, I had stepped back in time. The little girl looked at me as she was swept through the dancers and smiled at me. I nodded my head in acknowledgement. *What a great Dad!* I thought to myself, *that little girl looks so happy.*

"Brig!"

I could hear someone calling my name.

"Brig, time to get up!"

The ballroom started to ripple and become watermarked as my mind started to wake up to the reality of my life. No, I didn't want it to stop. I closed my eyes tighter, trying to crawl back to my dream, I wanted to dance, and I wanted to float.

"Brig!" My Mum yelled from the bottom of the stairs. I knew she'd keep going until I answered her.

"What!" Why can't she go away so I can go back to sleep? I could hear her footsteps gently climbing up the stairs. Argh, I threw the blankets up over my head. Of all the mornings, why can't I sleep in? A knock came next on my bedroom door. "I'm sleeping Mum."

The door squeaked gently open. "Brig" my Mum whispered. I could hear Winkles our cat meowing downstairs.

I threw the blankets off me in a huff. "What!"

My Mum smiled, "come on, get up."

"Why?" I moaned, "It's the weekend."

"We're going to Cargill's Castle this morning."

"What?"

"We're *all* going to Cargill's Castle this morning. I've someone meeting us there to let us through the fences."

"Mum, why?"

"What do you mean why? We're going on a family outing, and we're all going to have fun."

"Argh Mum" I moaned. "I don't want to go to stupid Cargill's Castle, I just want to sleep." I pulled my duvet back over myself and started to sink back down into bed.

She pulled the duvet back off me. "No way Brig, you're coming with us."

I sat up, rubbed my eyes and put on my best *not interested* face.

"Nope, not going to work, you're coming." She walked out the door and yelled behind her, "twenty minutes Brig, then we need to be out the door."

There was no getting out of this. Once my Mum had her mind set on something, it was set and there was no changing it.

I begrudgingly got into the car. It was late summer and the sun was still present, rain was forecast for the late afternoon, but my Mum in her determined manner was adamant that we would go to Cargill's Castle and we were all going to have an *awesome* time. I was 17 years old and have lived in Dunedin, New Zealand my whole life. I'd never been to Cargill's Castle, I'd heard of it, but never been, not even for school. It wasn't like the ruins of the great castles of Scotland or Ireland, but New Zealand was a relatively new country compared to them and Cargill's Castle was our equivalent and yet I'd never been. Isn't that always the way. You live in a place for so long and you never visit its historical landmarks. Well today we were going to this abandoned ruin and according to Mum, I was going to have *the time of my life*.

"Mum!" I yelled over Dad's loud county music.

She turned the volume knob down slightly. "Yeah?"

"Who are we meeting there?"

"Jason from work, I don't think you've meet him. His family owns some land that backs onto the castle. He's kindly said he'll take us through the fence so we can wander around and take a look. But guys, just letting you know that we shouldn't be doing this, its private property."

"What? Then why are we doing it?"

"Because we can and it's part of our heritage and we should learn about it."

I slumped back into my seat. There was no point arguing, we were on our way and now that I'd woken up a bit, I was a teensy bit excited about going to see the old place... not that I'd ever tell my Mum that especially after my protest this morning.

Dad pulled up beside a small round-about at the end of a cul-de-sac street by the St Clair Golf Course at the top of St Clair Hill. I could see the murky sea below the cliff in front of us. It was hauntingly beautiful.

"So where to now Alice?" My Dad asked.

Mum looked around. "I think his family lives in this house" she pointed to a peachy coloured house to the left of us which over looked the cliff. "Look, there's Jason."

We all looked to where she was pointing. An old man with grey thinning hair was waving frantically from out the top window. Mum waved back as she opened the car door.

"Righto, everyone out."

I got out and breathed in the fresh air. I could hear the waves crashing against the cliff and smelt the sea air. The sun was starting to come out and I could feel its warmth tickle my skin.

"Tom, leave it behind please."

"Aw Mum!" My brother whined.

"No, leave it."

"Fine!" He threw his iPad gently on the back seat of the car in protest. I rolled my eyes at him. He was a couple of years younger than me. We generally got on well, but lately he'd been so god dam moody. He had these crazy teenage hormones running through his body, which made him unpredictable and a bit of an ass. Unlike myself who was perfect. He poked his tongue out at me as he chased after Mum.

We followed Jason across a field of grass that flanked the cliff. I shoved my hands deep into my jean pockets and hunched my shoulders against the wind. Man it was windy up here. We stopped when we got to a tall wire fence. You could clearly see that people had been jumping or going under the wires trying to get a look at Cargill's Castle, some parts looked broken. It was a shame. It was tucked away and land blocked by private property. It was a landmark of Dunedin and my Mum felt it was important for people to see it. It was part of our history after all. Jason opened the tall wire gate and we went through. We walked into another field of grass flanking the cliff and stopped at an old stone fence. How awesome, I thought to myself.

"How cool is this fence! How did they get all those stones to stay there?" All the stones were lying on top of each other with nothing sticking them together. I mean it was a bit of a mess, there were rocks lying on the ground everywhere, but it was years' old and it was still standing, well partially standing.

"Great balance and hard work" Jason replied. Jason had on beige corduroy pants that were pulled up way too high. I smiled secretly to myself. So not cool, but he was old - he could get away with it.

I nodded my head as I imagined the men that would have placed all of these rocks into place. It wouldn't have been easy.

Dad, put his hand on my shoulder as we walked through the little wire gate that was placed in a section of the stone gate. I smiled up at him and walked through. There were huge weathered trees on this side of the fence all leaning inland. The leaves on the side to the sea had been stripped off by the wind. A shiver ran up my spine as we walked around to the front of the abandoned castle.

"Is this it?" Tom moaned.

Mum gave him a stern look then looked away ignoring him. "Wow, this would have been amazing back in its day."

Tom crossed his arms across his chest. "Yeah I suppose so."

"Why don't you go and have a look around."

It was certainly a castle, not your classic castle, but with its left-hand turret, it certainly fitted the description. I'd seen pictures of it a long time ago and I'd heard the story of Tunnel Beach where Mr Cargill made his servants chisel a tunnel by hand through a huge rock so his daughters could go to the sheltered beach that was below. The castle had been stripped completely bare of all its finery. No windows, no nothing, except spray painted graffiti all over its once majestic walls. It was made of a white greyish concrete that was now covered in cracks, moss, and gangster tags. It must've been a two story building at some stage, I could see the window shaped holes in the upper level. There were two large looking palm trees to the left of the tall turret with the rest of the vegetation taking over the landscape. There were large wide concrete stairs leading up to the main archway. This must've been the entrance.

"Cargill's Castle was originally known as The Cliffs at least that's what Edward Cargill wanted it to be called." Jason told us. "The Cargill's family helped make Dunedin what it is today."

My Mum nodded her head in acknowledgement.

"He was also elected the Mayor of Dunedin back in 1898."

"Was he? I did not know that" My Mum said.

"Yes, very influential and very clever, just like William Larnach was."

"Is that the man who built Larnach's Castle?" Tom asked. Larnach's Castle was another castle in Dunedin, on the Otago Peninsula, but unlike this one, Larnach's Castle had been well maintained throughout its long life. It was a huge tourist attraction in Dunedin and cost a small fortune to get in. I'd only been there once.

"Yes, the one in the same."

I looked out to the ocean, what a view! Imagine waking up in your castle bedroom every morning like a princess and looking out to the sea from your clifftop palace. "Such a shame it hasn't been looked after" I said, and I truly meant it as I kicked a rogue rock away from my foot.

"Yeah, but imagine the cost of doing that" my Dad piped in.

Jason nodded his head. "It proved to be too much for some, hence why it's been left to nature to look after it."

"Go, go and have a look around" my Mum pushed me forward, encouraging me to investigate. "We'll probably only be here once, may as well make the most of it."

I agreed this castle was very interesting. I was going to have a walk around and I was going to start by going up these stairs leading up to the entrance way.

As I moved toward them my mind blurred slightly. I shook my head to clear the fog. It wouldn't go away. I could feel a tug on my heart, a tug on my legs. I was being moved towards the archways, towards the stairs. I was floating, mesmerised by the intensity of wanting to touch the stone of the castle, to rub my cheek against its cold surface. I couldn't stop the pull. I had to touch it.

"Brigid!" my Mum yelled.

I could hear her calling me, but the pull was too strong, too intense. My eyes started to glaze over. I could see the building taking a new shape, a new façade, a new era.

"What's that on her arm?" I heard Tom call out.

I knew what it was, it always appeared in the sunlight. Normally if I'd been in the sun for too long or for too many days in a row, a discoloured pattern would appear on the lower part of my arm and gradually move like flames over my hand. It had always happened for as long as I could remember.

I felt arms wrap around me, holding me. "Brig, are you okay? Brigid?" My mother gently took my hand and held my arm up to look at what my brother was talking about. It was then that I snapped out of my hypnotic state and looked down. My breath left my lungs, the mark on my arm was glowing, dimly glowing, but glowing none the less… it had never done that before.

"What the..?" I shook my hand violently out of my mother's gentle grip trying to shake the glow out of it. "What the hell?" It wouldn't go, it started getting brighter. I screamed and starting running hysterically. "Get it off me, get if off!" My ears were buzzing, I was freaking out. I had to get this glow off my arm. I could hear my family yelling my name, reaching out to me but I wasn't listening. My heart thumped and my mind started to swirl. I stopped in my tracks and looked down at my arm again. It was still glowing – argh! I took off again towards the fence, screaming the entire way. I was turning into a lunatic, a raving bloody lunatic. Before I got to the trees, something stopped me. I stopped running, I couldn't explain it but it felt like I'd just ran into a brick wall but nothing was there. The hairs on the back of neck started to stand on end. What was going on? I looked down at my arm again and it was gone, the glow was gone. All that was left was the normal discolouration I have always dealt with throughout my life.

I felt my Dad come up behind me. He pulled me close to him as my tears streamed down his back and soaked his shirt. "What just happened?" I whispered.

He pulled me closer to his chest. "I don't know Brig, I don't know" he whispered back. He held me tight. "But we'll figure it out."

CHAPTER 2

There was a knock on the door. I looked at my bedroom door and groaned. I couldn't be bothered with my family right now.

"What!" I yelled, not bothering to hide my annoyance.

"Hey Brig, it's just me."

Relief hit me when I heard his voice. It was my best friend Hayden. He poked his head around the door and gave me a goofy smile.

I laughed. "Hey."

He jumped on the bed beside me and stretched out his legs. I was sitting in the middle of my double bed, surrounded by my baby pink comforter with my knees up to my chin, looking like a complete slob. "What's up?" He asked as he squeezed my shoulder. "You're sounding a tad grumpy this morning."

I looked at him and burst into tears. "I don't know, I have no idea what's going on?" I leaned my head on his shoulder and watched my blond wavy hair splay down the length of his chest.

He sighed and I felt the weight of his head on mine. "Tell me all about it Brig."

So I did, I told him about Cargill's Castle and how my world started to spin and drag me towards it. I told him about my arm glowing. He already knew what happened to my skin when I'm out in the sun for too long, but it had never glowed.

Once I'd finished, he fell silent. We both fell silent. I leaned closer into him and closed my eyes. I could smell his aftershave and it comforted me. "Are you sure it glowed?" he asked quietly.

I looked into his brown eyes. He was looking straight at me, holding my stare. "Yes" I replied. I jumped off the bed and sat in the chair beside my desk, slightly annoyed that he may not believe me. "Yes" I repeated, "my family saw it too." I threw my hands up in the air to emphasise the fact that I was not lying and what ever happened to me at Cargill's Castle was unexplainable.

"Alright, alright, I was just asking" he said quietly. He pulled himself over to sit at the side of the bed. The wooden floorboards creaked, protesting with the change of weight.

I put my head between my legs and started to rock. I needed to go to bed, to sleep and wake up again to start anew.

"Let's go there" Hayden said. "Let's go there this morning."

"What?" I asked in disbelief. "Are you serious? Why would I want to go back there?"

Hayden looked at me and smiled. "Because I want to see if your arm really does glow or if you're just telling me porkies." He stood up and poked me playfully in the ribs.

I stifled a laugh as he smiled at me and starting tickling me. "No fair, you know how much my ribs tickle."

He backed away and put his hands in the pockets of his denim jeans. I looked at his ruffled dark brown hair and back down to his now solemn eyes. "Seriously Brig, you should go back. I'll go with you, it may help you feel better."

"No way" I said. "There's no way I'm going back there."

I slowly walked up the stairs waiting for the pulling sensation to take over. I could feel Hayden's steady hand on my back, ready to grab me if anything happened. He was my best friend, my rock and I appreciated that he was here with me.

I closed my eyes as I took another step – nothing. Nothing was happening.

"I don't understand" I whispered to myself. I looked at Hayden "I don't feel anything."

"Are you okay?"

"I don't know." I looked at my arm, twisting it back and forth, nothing. "Maybe it was my imagination?"

"Maybe."

"But my parents were there, my brother was there, they all saw it."

"Brig, I don't know what to say, I wasn't there, but what I do know is that nothing is happening now, whatever happened before is in the past, maybe you should forget about it."

I looked into his brown eyes. He looked worried.

"Yeah maybe you're right. I should just forget about it." He was worried about me and I didn't want to upset him. He pulled me in close to his chest. I took a breath in and savoured his warmth. "Let's go home" I announced quietly feeling slightly deflated and embarrassed.

He tightened the hug momentarily then let go. "Sounds like a good idea, let's go, it's starting to get cold anyway."

As I reached the bottom of the steps I stopped. All the hairs on the back of my neck started to stand on end.

"You good?" Hayden asked.

My breathing stopped. I tried to listen. I could feel the panic taking hold. I remembered the worried look in his eyes earlier and didn't want to upset him again and in all honesty, I just wanted to go home. "Yip, all good, let's go." I didn't want to tell him that someone had just whispered my name. More like pleaded my name. I could still hear my name being whispered as we made our way back under the wire fence to Hayden's car. I closed my eyes and took a deep breath. I knew I was coming back here again – alone.

CHAPTER 3

I was walking through a meadow of long golden hay. Its softness brushed against my hands as I dragged them behind me. I could feel the sun on my back and I drew its energy into myself as it mixed with my blood and my mind, it exhilarated me. I could see the light glow from the patterns on my hand and I knew it was good, it was me and it was okay.

I walked to the path that lead towards the woods in total serenity, I was at peace. Tall trees flanked each side of the path, shadowing the ground, stopping the light from getting through. I closed my eyes as my wavy blond hair wisped behind me. I could hear wind chimes and whispers. I walked closer and stopped just before the shadows. I looked up lazily. The wind chimes I heard earlier were little bones tied to the branches of the trees gently knocking against each other, answering each other's calls. The darkness of the path called to me, beckoning me to walk through. I tried to take a step forward but my legs wouldn't move. They were heavy, I couldn't move. The wind got stronger, the bone's calls got louder, light exploded from my hand…. Brigid!

I sat up straight in my bed. Where was I? Sweat was pouring off me, my heart was pounding. I looked frantically around looking for something familiar, anything to anchor myself to my own world. My eyesight cleared from the dreamy haze and I saw my desk, my door, and the familiar walls to my bedroom. Tears rolled down my face with relief. What the hell just happened? That dream felt so real, I swear I was there in that meadow, I could still feel the wind in my hair. I pulled my duvet up and sunk back down in bed and closed my eyes. What's happening to me?

I wandered down the stairs aimlessly. Today was Monday, school day, totally not enthused about going to school today and I was so tired. I felt like I hadn't slept a wink all night.

I sat myself down on the stool furthest from my brother and huffed. I didn't want to go to school and I wanted my whole family to know about it.

"What's wrong with you?" Tom asked through a mouthful of Cocoa Pops.

I turned and gave him the evil eye as I poured some Weetie Bix bites into my plate ignoring him. I was not in the mood this morning.

"What?!" he yelled splattering Cocoa Pops all over the floor. "What was that for? Mum! Brigid is giving me the evil eye."

"Brigid, leave your brother alone" Mum bellowed out from behind the pantry door.

I just huffed and continued to eat my cereal giving my brother a cheeky smile in the process.

"Mum!" Tom whined.

"Enough!" she yelled. "Come on kids give me a break. Why can't you just get along? This is your last week of school before school holidays. Let's just get to the end of it okay."

I ignored her and my brother and finished my cereal. A knock at the door interrupted the tension in the room. I quickly grabbed my school bag knowing that it would be Hayden coming to pick me up. I swiped a couple of apples from the fruit bowl for my lunch and ran out the door mumbling my farewells.

I ran to Hayden's car and opened the door.

"Ready for another day in the pits?" he joked.

"Ready as I'll ever be" I replied glumly as I took a bite from one of my apples.

We sat quietly while I chewed away on my apple and listened to the radio. I was trying not to fall asleep, my eyes felt so heavy.

Hayden broke our long silence. "Looking a bit rough there Brig... Rough night?" he said light heartedly.

He started the car and petrol fumes from his old Mazda 323 wafted up my nose. I snuggled into the seat desperately wanting to be back in bed. "Yeah something like that" I replied. "I had the worst dream."

"Ohhh do tell."

"I seriously thought it was real."

"They're normally the best ones" he joked winking at me.

I laughed. I was deciding whether I wanted to tell him or not. For some reason I felt like it was my dream and my dream only. I told him anyway, he was my best friend. I told him about the hay, about the light glowing from the pattern on my hand, the bones in the trees and the shadows beckoning me to go down this dark path.

"It was weird" I finished off. Shivers went down my spine with the memory and my shoulders shook.

"That's strange Brig" he said with worry on his face. "That would explain the ugly big black bags under your eyes. It must've felt very real. Did it?"

He stopped the car in the school car park. I put my apple core in the plastic bag he left in his car for rubbish. "Yeah it did, it was really scary when I woke up. I couldn't snap out of it. I still felt like I was standing in front of these large trees."

"What did the trees look like?"

"They were huge, like pine trees I think?"

"Hmm, huge trees... could they have been oak trees not pine trees?"

"I don't know, I have no idea about trees, could have been oak trees - why?"

"I don't know, you said large trees, so I automatically thought of oak trees." He winked at me. "I know how bad you are with your flora and fauna."

"Hmm, yes I do suck, so yes maybe oak trees? But the weirdest thing was, I couldn't move. My legs were frozen. I felt like I was being pulled towards the path and I had to go down it, but something was stopping me."

He opened the door to the car and looked back at me. He had on his pale denim jeans and a tight black tee-shirt on. It stretched against his back muscles as he leaned to get out of the car. "Do you think you could have moved if you really tried?"

"No" I slammed the door closed wanting to forget about the whole dream. It unnerved me.

I swung my school bag over my shoulder as I walked beside Hayden. We both had Maths this morning, not my favourite subject, and I knew with school holidays approaching that there'd be a surprise math's quiz at some point throughout the week much to Mr Henderson, our math's teacher's, delight.

We walked in silence as we passed other kids on their way to school. I waved to a few of my friends but didn't stop. I wasn't in the mood for small talk. Hayden put his arm around my shoulder feeling my anxiousness. His warmth was comforting.

When we got to our class, Hayden gently turned me to face him and put his hands on my shoulders.

"Are you sure you couldn't move?"

"What?"

"Your dream, are you sure you couldn't move?"

"Yeah I couldn't move. Why do you keep asking me that?"

"No reason, right let's get this over and done with."

He pushed me gently in the direction of the door. I looked at it with dread and paused. Why was it not school holidays already?

Hayden walked in first just as the school bell rang.

"Heya Hayden" waved Alicia as she batted her eyelids and pushed out her chest as he walked past her.

"Argh" I thought to myself, she was so horrible. Alicia was one of the popular girls at school, with long straight brown hair and legs that went on forever. She ignored anybody who wasn't somebody at school. This included me. For some reason she had her eyes on Hayden, actually a lot of girls had their eyes on Hayden. He was a good looking guy with his short brown unruly hair and his teddy bear brown eyes, but I didn't see it. All I saw was my best friend Hayden. He ignored most of the attention he received by all the girls at school, instead he hung out with me.

Hayden nodded his head in acknowledgement to Alicia. She giggled and went back to writing in her school book. I gave Hayden a nudge, his face reddened as he took his seat beside me. I smiled, he was a mystery.

CHAPTER 4

It was near the end of the week and I couldn't wait for school to be out. I was looking at Mrs Lockhead writing her examples on the blackboard. I was taking nothing in, I was thinking about my dream last night. I closed my eyes and smiled. Last night's dream was completely different to my previous one. I was standing in the meadow of hay. I had on a long white dress with a long white lace train that was dancing aimlessly in the wind with my hair. There was a young man beside me holding my hand. His hand was warm and welcoming. We were both looking up into the sky with the sun on our backs. The feeling of belonging, warmth and revitalisation filled my body. It was heavenly. I looked at the man standing beside me. He began to turn to face me and then I woke up. Argh, I had woken up, why couldn't I have stayed asleep for a while longer. I needed to see him, needed to know him. I did notice one thing though, he had blond hair - mid length blond hair.

I felt a shove against my arm. I looked at Hayden in protest. He pointed to the front of the class. I stared at Mrs Lockhead while the rest of the class stared at me. I could feel my face redden.

"Well, do you know the answer Brigid?" Mrs Lockhead had her arms crossed over her robust belly and was tapping her foot impatiently. I could hear sniggering in the classroom.

"Um, can you repeat the question please?" I asked sheepishly.

"Keep your head out of the clouds Brigid and pay attention. The question was - what does a solar deity represent?"

Bugger, I didn't know. I'd done no homework this week. It was just about school holidays, what was the point? My face was as red as a beetroot. I shook my head, she frowned at me and turned her attention to Alicia who was waving her hand around in the air frantically.

"Yes Alicia."

"The Sun Mrs Lockhead, a solar deity represents the sun."

"Well done Alicia good to see some of the class haven't checked out yet for school holidays."

I looked at Alicia. She gave me a smug smirk and turned back around to the front of the class. Argh, she was annoying, of course the teacher had to ask Alicia and humiliate me in front of the whole class.

Hayden looked at me and I rolled my eyes in Alicia's direction. He laughed.

Hayden had been away from school for a while and I was getting worried about him. School was boring without him and I was so happy to finally see him. "How are you feeling?" I asked Hayden as we sat under a tree to eat our lunch. It was hot out and the tree offered solitude and protection from the sun, it was our happy place at school.

"Yeah alright I guess." Hayden said as he took a bite of his pie. He winced as the heat nearly scorched the roof of his mouth. "Still feel a bit rough, I picked the wrong butter chicken I guess."

"Jeez, that sucks. Well you haven't missed much. Oh, but the weirdest thing did happen to me the other day."

"Yeah?"

"Yeah, Alicia actually spoke to me."

"That is weird." He said with a cheeky smile then attempted to take another bite of his pie.

"Yeah she wanted to know where you were."

"Well, of course she did. She missed this handsome face around school, I can understand that." He winked at me.

I gave him a shove. "She wasn't the only one." I grabbed his arm and laid my head against it. I could feel the firmness of his bicep muscle. It had been lonely at school without him.

"Seriously, never be her boyfriend."

"Who - Alicia?"

I nodded.

"Why - someone jealous?"

I shoved him again. "No – it's just that you can do better."

He knuckle rubbed the top of my head messing up my hair. "Here's hoping that *better* comes along before I become desperate." He laughed.

I thought of the man in my dream, the one holding my hand in the meadow of hay and murmured, "yeah, me too."

"Hey Brig!" Kate called as she walked over to us. Kate was another one of our friends. She had brown hair, cut bluntly to her shoulders in a severe bob. She was an all-round good sort. We'd been friends since I could remember. She was the sort of person that everybody liked, including her teachers. I waved back and moved aside for her so she could sit down beside us under the tree.

"Hey" said Hayden.

"Hey, how're you feeling?" She asked Hayden.

"Still a bit yuck, but at least my face isn't hugging the toilet bowl."

She screwed up her petite nose. "Oeuw, too much information."

He smiled at her and pretended to throw up. She made a face at him and turned her attention to me. I was looking at my lunch which was not very exciting. I had a choice between a packet of raisins or an orange. "So Brig, are you going to join the archery club again next term? We could really use you. We have nationals coming up mid-year."

"Yeah probably." Kate got me into archery a couple of years ago. I loved it and I was strangely good at it.

"Great so I can sign you up again?"

"Yip absolutely." I said enthusiastically. I wouldn't miss nationals for the world.

"Great thanks Brig. How about you Hayden? You wanna join next term? We missed you this term."

"Nah, I'll give it a miss."

Kate and I looked at each other and rolled our eyes. Of course he didn't want to be a part of the archery team, or any team for that matter. Any team environment Hayden stayed away from. He was a bit of a rebel and didn't like to conform to the normal. If it wasn't for us he'd probably wander the school yard by himself while all the girls ogled him.

"Well if you change your mind let me know. I'll always make room for you."

"Thanks Kate. Hey what are you both up to after school?" Hayden asked.

We both shrugged.

"Come down to the beach with me. It's so hot."

Kate and I looked at each other and squealed in unison "Hell yes." We both giggled as Hayden rolled his eyes at us.

"If you're going to squeal like that I'm going to uninvite you both."

I stroked the side of his face "Oh, come on don't be like that Hayden Wayden. You know you love us and life would be boring without us."

"Yip my life would be a lot different without you." He looked straight into my eyes and held the stare. I couldn't decide what that meant or why he was looking at me so intensely. I shoved him gently in response and he stopped staring.

The sun was beaming. What a day it was. We were down at St Kilda Beach below the sand dunes. We had our towels laid out and we were all flopped on top of them. I had my short denim shorts and my red bikini top on. Kate had her denim shorts on too, but a pink singlet on top. Hayden had his board shorts on with no top on. Hayden had a good set of Abs.

I opened my eyes lazily and watched the families with their children. People were walking their dogs and students were playing beach cricket further down the beach. Life was good at this moment. I loved the sun and the beach. I loved summer and I loved my friends. I looked down at my arm, no discolouration yet, I hadn't been in the sun long enough for that to happen yet. I laid back and enjoyed the sun again. I day-dreamed about the man that held my hand in the sun. There was a connection I was sure of it. There was something there, I knew it was just a dream and I couldn't wait to go to sleep tonight.

"Hey Brig" Hayden gave me a gentle shove.

"What?" I slurred.

"Check it out?" He was pointing to a group of girls and in the middle of the group was Alicia, prancing around in her teensy tiny bikini and yes she did look amazing.

"So?" I said "who cares." I closed my eyes again. I could feel Hayden's smile through my closed eyelids. He knew the parade was for him and he also knew that it annoyed me, she annoyed me.

Kate had fallen asleep. When we finally decided to leave I woke her up. She stood up still in a daze. I started laughing. "Oh no Kate."

"What? What?!" she asked looking around herself frantically, disorientated.

Hayden looked at Kate and started laughing too. "We might need to come back to the beach tomorrow so you can do the other side."

I put my hand to my mouth and tried not to laugh.

"What, what is it?"

"Kate you're sunburnt." I told her gently.

She looked down at her red thighs, she cringed. "Aw that's gonna hurt? Why do I always do this to myself?"

We laughed together all the way to Hayden's car, especially when she took her sunglasses off and displayed the white rings around her eyes. He dropped Kate off first and then me.

"Do you want to come in before you head home?" I asked him.

He stopped the car and took the keys out. "Yeah why not, Tom promised to slaughter me in a game of Sonic the Hedgehog anyway. I'll do that before I head home."

I laughed as I got out the car. Hayden ended up staying for dinner and Tom held true to his promise and slaughtered him in Sonic the Hedgehog much to Hayden's disgust. It was a good day and yes, my dreams that night we filled with light, warmth and a gentle man's hand within my own.

CHAPTER 5

I stood staring at the concrete façade of Cargill's Castle. It was early morning and nobody was there. My Dad had asked me where I was going at the crack of dawn, I told him I was going for a run. He'd looked at me strangely but accepted it. He knows that I don't run. I hated lying to my father, but this had to be done. I gave him a hug before I left.

I had to come again and this time it had to be by myself. I remembered the looks on my families and Hayden's face the last time I came with them, it was not good. I didn't want to put them through that again and I didn't want them to see me turn into a looney if that's what I was becoming. It was early Saturday morning and yes, it was finally the school holidays. Today was the day I was finally going to find out what was going on. These dreams, my arm glowing and Cargill's Castle were all connected, I could feel it in my bones and I needed to find out why. I walked slowly towards the concrete stairs. I started to feel the familiar pull, the tug towards the archway. I looked down at my arm, it started to glow. It was happening. My heart started to pulse and my vision blurred. I fell to my knees as they buckled beneath me. "I can do this, I can do this" I whispered to myself, I hung my head and tried to clear the blurriness in my mind. "Get it together

Brigid" I encouraged myself. The glow was spreading like flames to my hand. The pull to touch the stone was immense. I stopped fighting it. I braced my legs and stood up. The pulse of the light was pulling me, pulling me to a place unknown but familiar. I drifted up the stairs and stopped at the top. There was a smell, a smell of flowers, of spring. I could hear my name being called over and over again. Gently, it was being gently spoken, a beckoning, someone needed me. I held my hand up, I had to touch, had to feel the pulse from the wall.

As I touched the wall, a flash of light burst from my hand. The energy was intense, but it felt good. I could see the stone melt away, the light was spiralling and trying to pull me though the stone. A hand shot out from the light. I grabbed it. I knew I needed to grab it. Everything spun, it was spinning me around, spinning me, stretching me, bending me. I couldn't hang on much longer. I could see blond hair in front of me, an assurance everything was going to be okay. I felt safe. I held on for as long as I could until I passed out. The next thing I saw was a face, a male's face, a devastatingly handsome male face with blond mid-length hair staring into my eyes. I took a deep breath. I put my hands up and felt his face. Yep, it felt real. I closed my eyes and opened them again. He had a smile on his face this time.

"Hello" he said.

I sat up with a fright and whacked my head with his. I passed out again.

I moaned. My head pounded and I felt like I needed to throw up. I could feel the ground under my hand and remembered what had happened. The blond man! I sat up quickly.

"Easy my lady, remember what happened last time."

I opened my eyes and spied my blond dream-man holding his forehead smiling at me. He looked to be the same age as me.

I cringed. OMG I nearly knocked out my dream-man, how embarrassing. I decided to not go there and sat up. "Where am I?"

"You Brigid are where you are supposed to be. Quick we don't have much time, come with me before they find you."

I could feel his urgency. "Who? Who will find me?"

He grabbed my arm and pulled me up. "We need to get you to the oak trees, they can't find you there, quick."

I stalled. "What are you talking about? Who are you? Who's after me?" I looked into his pale blue eyes and I could feel my knees buckle. I knew who he was - he was the man from my dreams.

"You are in immense danger my lady, you need to come with me and quickly." He started to pull my arm to follow him.

"What? Are you mad? I, I, I have no idea where I am or who you are? I'm not about to follow you to the oak trees, or whatever that is." I exclaimed. His eyes were awesome.

"You took my hand, are you not already following me?"

I quickly looked around at my surroundings. I was in the middle of some town square. There was a fountain. I could hear the running of water. It was a town, a medieval looking town. Everything looked grey and glum. There were no leaves on the trees, no noises, no birds, and no people. He was right, I was already following him.

"Where am I?" I asked again.

He moved closer to me as he wrapped his arm around my waist. My heart raced. "I'll explain later. You need to move now… now!"

I started to run, I felt his urgency, and I ran. I ran behind him as he dragged me along the dirt hardened streets. No one was around, it must've been early in the morning there to, where ever we were. This all felt too surreal. He turned his head and put his finger to his mouth, motioning for me to keep quiet. I ran quietly behind, mistrusting my eyes. My dream-man was wearing a green leather skirt held together with a thick gold belt. His blond hair was loose and bounced around as he ran. He had wide leather bands around his ankles and wrists with a symbol of the sun etched into them. He had a shield strapped to his back which also had the emblem of the sun on it. His broad, muscular shoulders and arms moved on either side of the shield as he ran and his top half was naked, completely naked for all to see. I think I was officially going mad. I was running behind what looked like a god.

He stopped suddenly. I nearly banged into his shield. "What?" I asked. I was happy I wore my running gear this morning or this would not have worked.

"Shh, we need to walk slowly from here. We could be sensed if we flee too fast."

He grabbed my hand and looked into my eyes. "Trust me, I would never harm you, trust me."

Before I could think, I was already telling myself I trusted him and followed him like a little lost lamb. What would Hayden think if he saw me in my current predicament? He'd be howling with laughter I was sure of it. I grimaced, but I was sure I was doing the right thing. We kept going in silence, dodging the rare person that came across our path. After a while I could see the large trees in the distance from my dream, they must be the Oak trees. Hayden was right. My arm started to glow, I could feel it race down my arm to my hand, the same hand that my dream god was holding. He jerked when the glow hit his. He stopped and looked at me and smiled. "Run" he said.

"What?"

"Run! Run now!" I could hear movement from the hay. I bolted, he quickly followed. I knew this was not good. I could feel shots of air whizzing past my ears. What was going on? I turned to see my dream god block our behinds with his shield. Someone was firing something at us. I couldn't see who or what they were firing. I faced the oak trees and ran faster, still thankful for my Lycra running pants and Nike running shoes.

I stopped just before the path to the oak trees. I couldn't move. I saw the familiar little bones hanging on the trees, singing their little songs. I froze. I was cemented to the ground.

"I can't move" I said. "I can't move past this point." I looked at my dream god as my heart starting racing. I tried again but it was like my dream, I couldn't move, I was stuck.

He took my hand and looked into my eyes. "Breath, close your eyes and breath. Let your light shine, breathe, and let your light find its way home. You are the light Brigid. Imagine your light creating a door, open it and walk through."

I breathed as he held his shield up high and deflected a shot to my head. I did my best to ignore it. I had to get to past this point. I willed the light, the glow from my arm to shine. Shine, come on shine. I could feel the flow coming, it was happening. The light was blinding. He pushed me over the threshold. All the panic, all the whizzing, everything stopped. I could hear the birds chirping, I could feel the light from my dream. It was sanctuary.

I turned to see him leaning over me again. "You need to tell me what is going on? I have dreamt of you, of all of this, this is not right but yet it is."

"You Brigid are our saviour, my…"

My vision started to blur, my light went out. I could see concrete it was spinning and melting, I was getting pulled back. "No!" I shouted, "No!"

CHAPTER 6

I could feel the cold ground underneath me. My head pounded. "What?" I whispered to myself, "What just happened?"

"Brigid!"

I opened my eyes as I heard my name being shouted. It was a familiar voice, it was Hayden. My vision started to clear but my head was still pounding. I felt strong arms wrap around me. "Oh Brig, thank god!"

I was sitting in the middle of a crude stone circle with Hayden's arms wrapped around me. All different sized pebbles and rocks secured the circle containing me with four lit candles sitting in four exact areas of the circle. "What? Hayden!" Realisation hit me. "What are you doing?" I was back at Cargill's Castle.

"Lucky I was here Brig or you may have been stuck there."

I pulled away from his embrace. "What are you doing here Hayden?" I was annoyed, annoyed at being pulled back before I figured out what everything was about. I never found out who that man from my dreams was, why we were being chased and more importantly, why my arm glowed. He said I was their saviour, whose saviour? He knew my name. How did he know my name? He was about to say something else, but this numbskull interfered. "Well?!" I blurted out. I looked at his sincere look and took a deep breath, it wasn't his fault, he thought he was saving me. "Look I'm sorry, thank you." I said solemnly "thank you for coming." I started to stand up as Hayden gave me a lift from under my arms. I shook and wiped off the loose dirt from my running clothes. Something dawned on me. The circle, the candles, Hayden? "Hayden, you still haven't answered me. Why are you here and why am I standing in the middle of this circle?" I held my head and felt the bump on my forehead from colliding with my dream man. Mortification came quickly to my mind as I remembered how I'd nearly knocked him out, how embarrassing.

"First off, you are welcome even if you don't sound like you mean it and second, we need to talk."

I glanced at the circle again, "yes we do."

I helped Hayden put the rocks back in silence and we made our way back to his car. The wind was picking up and I pulled the hood over my head as I got in the car. "Right, talk."

"Okay, this is all going to sound really weird, so keep an open mind." He smiled as he squeezed my knee.

"I'm starting to get a bit freaked out now Hayden, tell me. Do you know why my hand glows?" I pulled my knee away from his hand.

He looked out the window, obviously hurt by my actions. "That's certainly part of it for sure," I sat forward in the passenger seat. I knew I wanted to hear this, but why would Hayden know and why has he not told me before.

He turned back around to me. "First of all, I wasn't sure it was you?"

"What wasn't me?

"I wasn't sure it was you until you told me your hand glowed. Brig, do you know much about the gods? The Greek Gods, the Celtic Gods, those types of gods?"

I shook my head "No, not really."

"Well Brig, I believe you somehow have the life force of The Great Mother, The Lady of the Sacred Flame running through your veins – Brigid" he announced as he held his hands up to emphasize the claim.

"Brigid? There's a god called Brigid? With the same name as me?"

"It would appear so, which is very strange that your parents decided to call you that. Maybe they subconsciously knew."

"Knew what? Who is this Brigid, I have never heard of her and why do I have her running through my veins and more importantly how do you know?" I'd heard of Thor and Zeus, but not Brigid. I was interested to find out what my best friend had been holding back from me all of these years.

He took a deep breath. "I'll tell it as I remember it and I'll condense it a little bit so you don't get overwhelmed. Righto, you ready?"

I took a deep breath and nodded. I wasn't totally sure if I was ready for it, but I don't think I had a choice.

"Okay, so Brig, The Great Mother Brigid was married to a half demon-god, Bres. Bres was from an enemy family. The marriage was made to bring the families closer together and to avoid any more fighting. Bres was from the Fomorians, the sea people and she of the

Danu people. They lived together happily for a while. They had three sons together - Ruadan, Luchar and Uar. Over the years, Bres became a tyrant in his rule and the Danu people renounced him and sent him back to the sea. Bres took his sons he had with Brigid with him. Ruadan, the eldest son came out of the sea a few days later by his father's command and killed a sacred tribe member of the Danu people as revenge. Ruadan died for his efforts. Brigid's roar of sadness and betrayal was heard all other the worlds. Her pain and loss was immense. Her husband's family turned completely against her and plotted her demise. Anyway, to cut a long story short, before they turned her into stone and froze her in time, in her rage and grief she released some of her light into the universe, the light that made her Brigid, the lady of the sacred flame. This light was destined to attach itself to someone's soul, but the Fomorians have been chasing it and bouncing it away before it can take hold, until 17 years ago. The light stopped. Some thought the flame had burned out, some believed it had found its home. I wasn't sure."

I sat there dumbfounded. I think he lost me at married to a half demon-god. Everything from that point sounded like gibberish.

He waved a hand in front of my face "Brig? Brig? Earth to Brig? Did you get any of that?"

I looked at him with disbelief. "Ah, not really."

He retold his story as I sat there jiggling my legs, utterly dumbfounded. This can't be true and if it was, what has Hayden got to do with it all?

We both sat silent in the car listening to the drumming of my knees gently banging together, a nervous twitch. "Okay, so I have the light of a goddess in me... right?"

"That would be right."

"Why?"

"Why what exactly?"

The wind started to pick up and gentle rain drops hit the windows of the car. "Why do I have her light inside me? Why did it go into me?"

"All I know is that Brigid knew seconds before she was turned to stone by the Fomorians that this was the end and she'd be dammed if this was it, so she shot out some of her life force from her body and whispered a spell for it to find a baby born at daybreak and to bring the glow back to her. Brigid, you are the saviour, you've been destined to save a Goddess and not just any goddess, Brigid, the lady of the sacred flame."

The Saviour, I'd heard that before. The boy from my dreams mentioned that also. "The saviour" I laughed out loud. "Me" I pointed to myself. "I can't be the saviour, I can hardly save myself. How the hell am I supposed to save a Goddess?" I held my side to stop my laughter. I wiped my eyes. This was ridiculous.

"Brig, this isn't funny, this is serious."

"Actually coming to think of it Hayden, how do you know all of this? How did you know I was at Cargill's Castle and how did you know how to bring me back from wherever I was?" I looked at him intensely. He had some explaining to do.

He took a big gulp and put his seat belt on. The rain was hammering down now. "Look, how about we go and get some breakfast and I can explain my side of things."

At the sound of the word *breakfast* my stomach betrayed me and let a huge rumble rip. "Okay, let's go, but it's your shout."

Hayden turned the car on and put his windscreen wipers on high. I texted Mum to let her know where I was going. She texted back asking for a doggy bag of the shortbread hearts they always had in their cabinet. I couldn't help but smile as Hayden drove away at my Mum's text, of course she did.

I took a large gulp of my banana smoothie. I was anxiously waiting for my pancakes to arrive, but the banana smoothie Hayden so nicely *shouted me* was filling the gap nicely. We managed to get a seat on the bar leaner facing the road towards St Clair beach. People's voices filled my ears. I closed my eyes and listened to the voices and the rain that was hitting the window. There was nothing better than being warm and eating good food when it was wet and windy outside. It gave me the warm fuzzies.

Hayden returned from the toilet, sat down beside me and took a big gulp of his iced chocolate. "Right, so you want to know why I know all of this and that I'm not a complete loon?"

"Sure do, in fact I can't wait to hear what you have to say." I smiled sarcastically at him. A feeling of betrayal filled me and I didn't care that his hurt emotions showed on his face. I needed answers, answers from him.

"Okay, so – to put it bluntly, I'm your protector."

I spurted out my banana smoothie and grabbed my napkin to clean it up. "You're my what?"

"I'm your protector. At least that is what I'm supposed to be."

"*My* protector? Are you serious?"

He took my hands in his. They were cold and clammy, he was nervous. "My whole existence has been to make sure you survive and to make sure the light continues to glow."

I pulled my hands away from him. "Are you serious?"

"Totally serious? I'm a demi god Brig, a minor deity. I've been searching for you for a very long time and I'm glad I found you first. I wasn't sure, but I was pulled here to Dunedin, New Zealand. Everything I have done or been, it's because of the pull I have to you, to The Mother's glow. I knew that when you stayed out in the sun too long your arm and hand started to discolour into a pattern and I thought that maybe that was enough, but when you said you glowed, well I knew then."

I remembered telling him, and he did seem to believe me and then he went to Cargill's Castle with me. He seemed supportive. Maybe he was telling the truth. "Brig, I'm a descendant from Brigid the lady of the flame and my whole purpose has been to find you and keep you safe from the Fomorians."

"The Fomorians? They are after me?"

"Yes they are and have been for centuries. They will stop at nothing to defeat Brigid and end her forever. They also felt betrayed that Bres was denounced as king and sent back to the sea. They need their revenge."

"Well I'll be damned." I blurted out. "So, my hand glows because of her light inside me and this light is destined to find its way back to her?"

"Well no, the light needs to continue to glow. It doesn't necessarily have to find its way back to her. The Danu's believe that her life force is still present as long as it glows within someone, something. That is enough. The war that would follow after her return would be catastrophic and they don't want that to happen. They have found peace, they are at peace."

I was starting to believe him, maybe this was true. Hell, my arm did glow. He always had my back when things got tough, stuck by me no matter what. "So this place that I went to." It dawned on me as I said it that we hadn't even talked about that yet, he hadn't even asked. "There was a man, a gorgeous man that pulled me though the concrete of the castle." I watched him to see his reaction. He frowned, I continued. "He said some people were after me, which would be the Fomorians right? He made me run through a town towards some oak trees."

"Did you go through? Did you walk through the oak trees?"

I lied "No, no I couldn't I was stuck." I don't know why I lied but there it was.

He put a reassuring hand on my shoulder. The feeling of betrayal was starting to leave my body and a sense of security replaced it. "The man you are talking about would no doubt be Cichol, also a demi-god, but he is on the side of the Fomorians, the ones that want you dead. What did he say to you?"

"He just said that people were after me and I had to run. He also mentioned something about me being the saviour too… that's all I got before you pulled me back."

"Lucky I was there when I was. I'd hate to think what he would have done to you."

Hayden's words worried me. I'd never been scared of him in my dreams. "It didn't feel like that, I didn't feel like I was in danger. It felt like he was trying to help me."

"Lies, all lies. Brig, Cichol would do anything to trap you and burn that light out of your body. He managed to get you through his portal to his evil world, he'll stop at nothing. He can't be trusted. He's the enemy Brig. He'll say and do anything for you to believe he is on your side and when you least expect it…" he trailed off as he took a mouthful of eggs.

A shiver went up my spine at his unspoken words. I leaned away from Hayden as my pancakes were served to me. I thanked the waitress and grabbed my fork and started to dig in. As I ate, I contemplated what Hayden had said. Was my dream-man my enemy? I didn't want to believe it, but it was like Hayden said, he'd stop at nothing. At that moment I felt like going to bed and eating loads of ice-cream to heal my broken heart.

"Brig, promise me something." Hayden asked with his mouthful.

"Yeah what?" I replied with just as big a mouthful as what he had.

"Never go back. Never risk it again. Too much is at stake. I can keep you safe. I know how to keep you safe. The Danu people are happy, they're at peace – let's just leave it at that."

CHAPTER 7

I took the shortbread hearts back home to Mum. It was still reasonably early and I still had most of the day ahead of me. Mum was in the kitchen drinking her coffee, enjoying the little bit of sun she'd found poking out from behind the rain.

"Hey Mum."

"Hey Brig."

I gave her the paper bag filled with her biscuits. "Yum thanks Brig, love these. How much do I owe you?"

"Nothing, it was Hayden's shout."

She raised her eyebrows, "well tell Hayden I'm very grateful." She opened the bag and broke a bit off. "Yum!" She shoved it into her mouth. "Want some?"

I held my stomach. I was so full. "No thanks. I had a mountain of pancakes and I'm full as a bull."

"Great, more for me" she murmured as she shoveled some more into her mouth.

I went round to the kitchen and put the jug on. "Want another one Mum?"

"No thanks, I'm good. Look Brig, I've been meaning to talk to you, I've been so busy lately that I haven't really had a moment to do it."

This can't be good I thought to myself. "Yes, what do you want to talk about?" I poured the milk and coffee into my cup and waited for the water to boil.

"Come sit down when you're ready."

"Right" I replied. I willed the jug to take it's time. I'd been up early this morning, doing my adventuring and going through portals and stuff, I was tired. I hoped I wasn't in any kind of trouble. I racked my brain to see if I could remember anything that I may have done to get me in trouble lately.

The jug boiled to my dismay, I poured it into my cup and stirred it until it was all mixed together. "Right, I'm here, what do you want to talk about?" I sat down beside her.

"I want to know if you're alright."

"Yeah, I'm okay."

"How are you feeling about the other day, the day at Cargill's Castle? Look, I know how freaked out you were, I think we all were, but I want you to know that we can work through this together."

I smiled, if only she knew. "Thanks Mum I appreciate it. I was worried about it, but now not so much, it's all good, just something I have to deal with I suppose."

"Well you don't have to deal with it by yourself. Your father and I are always here for you."

I took a sip of my coffee and felt the familiar warmth make its way down my throat. I wondered if I should tell her. She'd be able to help me, or would she think I was crazy and how would she handle Hayden's claim about being my protector. I wondered exactly how old Hayden was. Was Hayden even his real name? I felt my heart racing and tried to slow it down. "Thanks Mum. Hey Mum, why did you call me Brigid?" Mum looked at me slightly surprised by the question. She had her long brown hair tied back into a loose bun at the bottom of her neck. Her blue eyes were the same as mine and I saw them widen just slightly with my question.

"Well," she broke another bit of biscuit off and put it into her mouth. She finished chewing it before she answered. "It was weird, you were originally supposed to be called Veronica but just as I was giving birth to you the name Brigid came to my mind, in fact a lady with a head full of flames came to my drugged fuelled mind repeating the word Brigid over and over again, and it stuck, you were to be called Brigid much to your father's dismay but I wasn't budging." She smiled at me and gently stroked my face with her hand. "I had to call you Brigid, it felt wrong if I didn't."

I smiled at her. Little did she know that it probably wasn't a drug fuelled image, but an actual image of Brigid herself, goddess of the sun. "Well, I like it, thanks Mum and thanks to the drugs that changed your mind from Veronica to Brigid."

She laughed. "Seriously Brig, do you want to go see a doctor or something?"

I looked at my hand and pulled my sleeve down over it. "No, I think its okay. I'm okay. I have come to terms with it." I saw the worry in my Mum's face. "Unless of course it starts to make me feel unwell or something? Then I can go see a doctor. But I feel good. I'm good Mum."

The worry was still in her face, but a smile was also there. "I'm always here sweetheart, always."

"I know Mum, thanks. How was your biscuit?"

"Amazing!" We both laughed at the empty paper bag sitting on her lap. I emptied the rest of my coffee in to the sink and went to leave as I heard the car pull up under the house, which meant Tom was home. I needed solitude at the moment. "Hey Brig, did you know you were born exactly at daybreak?"

I stopped dead in my tracks. My heart sped up. This is all very real, why me? "Wow, that's amazing Mum, maybe that's why I'm so awesome!"

"Totally" she replied.

When I got to my room, I shut the door and opened up my laptop. I had some researching to do. The first thing I goggled was *Brigid the Goddess,* and wow! She was one busy goddess. She was known as lots of names, Bride, Bridey, Brighid, Brigit, Briggidda, Brigantia, The Great Mother, and Goddess of the Sacred Flame. She was the patroness of healing poetry, smith craft, inner healing, vital energy, light, fire to name a few. They even have a shrine at Kildare, Ireland for her, or should I say the Christian version of her. She was a warrior and a maiden, aligned with fire and water. She even has her very own festival named after her, St Brigid's Day, something to do with the spring and bringing light after the winter's darkness. She sounded like she was a bit of everything and represented females everywhere with her spirit, love and honour. How was *I* supposed to save this amazing person, I mean amazing Goddess. I wasn't amazing, I was just little old Brigid from Dunedin, New Zealand. I flopped myself on the bed and phoned Kate.

"Hey girl, how are ya?"

I gave an exaggerated sigh "Okay I guess. What are you up to? I've had a full on day. Wanna go do something?" I needed some Kate time to cheer me up.

"Yeah absolutely, what did you have in mind and why so morbid?"

"No real reason, just tired I guess. Wanna meet me at school and do some archery practice, blow off some steam."

"Yeah totally keen. You okay? It's the school holidays, you should be on a school free high. I know I am."

"Yeah I am, I'm just... tired or need some exercise or something. Meet you there in thirty minutes?"

"Sweet, see you soon." Kate had the key to the gym thanks to her Mum being the president of the school PTA Board.

I took a deep breath and slowed my heart rate down as I pulled the bow string to my anchor, the side of the mouth. I looked at the target and released. Bullseye.

"I wouldn't expect anything less from you Brig." Kate said as she pulled her bow string back to make her shot. I didn't answer her, I didn't want to stuff up her shot. She hit just out of the bullseye. "Bugger!"

"That's still good Kate, I wouldn't worry about it."

"Brig, you've only been doing this for a couple of years, and what's worse, I taught you. You're now officially better than me." Kate pouted.

In all fairness I was getting better than her, but I wasn't about to admit it to her face. What sort of friend would that make me? I shot the rest of my arrows, most got within the first yellow circle, with one getting in the second. Not bad, I thought to myself. "There's something so relaxing about shooting an arrow." I said to Kate after she shot her last arrow.

"I know, I love it - It's good for the soul. There's nothing better than the sound of your arrow slicing into the target."

"Totally! Want to go again? I might push mine back further."

Kate nodded her approval. We grabbed our arrows and pushed back our targets and lined up to do it again.

"Do you believe in God?" I blurted out.

"What? God?"

"Yeah, but not Jesus Christ God, but the old gods like Zeus and Thor and stuff?"

"I don't know, I've never really thought about it. Do you?"

"Not sure." That kind of was the truth. I wasn't certain that the gods definitely existed, I'd never seen any, but I was on the verge of believing, what with my glowing arm and stuff. That's pretty good evidence that something existed that was beyond belief.

"Well Brig, I don't know for sure if they exist but I do know something. Normally myths are based on some sort of truth, a true story that's been exaggerated so much that it's too wild to believe."

"Yeah I suppose you're right."

"Do you think vampires are real?" Kate asked with her eyes wide open.

We both sniggered. "No" I answered. "Definitely not." Doubt filled me though, jeez if Goddess's were actually real, could vampires or werewolves be real too? I hoped not.

"Nah vampires aren't real."

We both jumped and put our hands on our hearts. Mine was pumping. "Hayden!" I yelled, "Don't scare us like that, jeez."

"Hayden seriously, don't surprise a girl that's just about to shoot an arrow." Kate mumbled as she pointed the bow and arrow at him.

Thank god, I secretly thought to myself with relief. If anyone knew if vampires existed it would be Hayden and I was happy they didn't. One less thing to worry about.

He laughed and gently pushed it away. "Sorry ladies, I didn't mean to scare you, just wanted to join the conversation and for arguments sake, vampires are not real."

"We know that Hayden." I rolled my eyes as I prepared myself to shoot my arrow. I slowed my breath and imagined the arrow hitting the point of the target I was aiming for and released.

"Getting good Brig," Hayden said.

"Yeah she's been hitting bullseyes all day." Kate said as she released her arrow. "Bugger" she said as she watched her arrow hit the outer circle. "Hayden you're putting me off."

"Ha, not my problem you can't aim straight."

Kate punched him in the arm.

I ignored them both and took aim again. I had two arrows left and then I'd call it a day. I breathed slowly looking at the target. My breath caught in my throat as I felt a rush of air fly past my face. I looked at the arrow splitting my arrow down the middle. I turned to Hayden with my mouth wide open.

He gave the bow back to a stunned Kate and smirked. "What?" he laughed as he shrugged his shoulders.

"Hayden you totally need to come to Nationals with us," Kate squeaked. "We would win for sure!" She started jumping up and down clapping her hands. He just smirked at her. He had no intention of going to Nationals with us.

I on the other hand was fuming. He'd split my arrow in half. "Hayden, you split my arrow."

"Oh, you saw that." He joked.

I shoved him, "and you gave me a fright you big oaf."

He laughed as he pulled me into a tight hug. He swayed me gently to and fro and giggled. I couldn't help it and started laughing myself.

"Seriously Hayden, you are good, we need you" Kate pleaded.

He just laughed.

Kate pouted. "Fine, but if we lose I'm blaming it on you."

Hayden held his arm out for Kate too. "Come on, bring it in. You need a hug too."

She smiled and didn't resist as Hayden pulled her in to the group hug. I could smell his aftershave and Kate's conditioner in her hair. I smiled. I loved these two.

CHAPTER 8

I'd just finished dinner and made my way upstairs to my room with a cup full of unsalted mixed nuts. I put the cup down on my white study desk. I threw myself on my bed and pulled the comforter up. It was still light outside even though it was 8.00pm at night. I loved summer. If this was winter it would have been dark by now. I was pooped. It had been a big day. I replayed the day in my head. 1 – Went to another world and found my dream man there. 2 – Got sucked away from my dream man by my best friend. 3 – My best friend tells me he is my protector because I have the light of a goddess in my body. 4 – I did some archery training with Kate. 5 – the most important one… I'm supposed to be some sort of saviour and my dream man is out to kill me. What a day. I closed my eyes as I felt my heart slowing. I needed to sleep and I hoped that my dreams would be happy ones and that my dream man would not make an appearance, especially if he wanted me dead. All this excitement has made me tired.

I stretched as I slowly woke up. It was dark outside. I grabbed my phone and checked the time. 10.00pm. I licked my lips and went on a hunt for my bottle of water. I found it on the floor at the end of my bed. I took a big sip as I looked out at the moon shining through my window. It was a full bright moon tonight. It was beautiful. I wondered if there's a moon goddess. If there was a sun goddess, there must be a moon goddess. I wondered if they would be sisters or at least friends. Maybe they are enemies. I shook my head, I didn't care whether they were friends or even if there was a moon goddess, I wanted those mixed nuts I'd left on the study desk beside my bed, I was hungry.

"What!" I looked down at my cup of nuts. It was tipped over and most of the nuts were gone. I straightened the cup up. "Tom," I whispered under my breath, "you little weasel stole my nuts." I whizzed out of my room to confront him. All the lights were out in the house and no light was coming from his room. Everyone was asleep. This can wait until the morning I thought to myself or I can get some revenge I smiled to myself mischievously. What could I do? Ah, who was I kidding, I'd just talk to him tomorrow about it, I wasn't that adventurous, or I could hide his PlayStation. I smiled again to myself, he would hate that.

I made my way back to my room and got changed into my pyjamas. They were my favourite. Big white pyjamas with lots of different coloured hearts on them. There was a silk draw string at the waist of the pants and I tied them up loosely. I sat at the end of the bed looking at the empty cup of nuts. I really wanted them, Tom was such a pain. I noticed a pile of nut crumbs up on my lower shelf which sat above my desk. It housed my smaller novel books. I stood up and touched the crumbs. I grabbed some between my fingers and brought them up to my nose and sniffed. Yip it was definitely nut crumbs. I looked up at the next shelf up. The same thing. Why would Tom leave a trail of nut crumbs on my shelves? Why didn't he just take the whole cup? That's what I would have done. The trail stopped at that top shelf. I opened my jewellery box that lived up there. It used to make music as the ballerina spun around but that's been broken for a long time now. Nothing except for my little trinkets I normally leave in there. I moved some of my books that were also up there. I didn't know what I expected to find. It's all too weird. I pushed it to the back of my mind and grabbed my book and settled back into my bed to a long reading marathon. I settled down and turned to the page I'd folded over to mark my place the previous night. I don't know how long I'd been reading for but my eyes were starting to get tired. I turned my head towards my study desk.

Crunch.

What was that? I could hear crunching coming from my desk. I stopped breathing so I could hear properly.

Crunch, crunch...

What the? I sat up slowly and gently put my book down. I was definitely awake now. I tip toed over to my desk and stopped to listen...

Crunch, crunch, crunch.

I gently lifted the lid of my jewellery box and peered in. Just my trinkets and nut crumbs. Nut crumbs! What was going on? I turned on my light. We had a mouse in the house. We must have, what else would make that noise and steal my nuts. I must admit we do get mice sometimes in the winter when it's cold outside, but I have never seen them or heard of them eating a whole cup of nuts in summer. I dropped the lid down again. I'm going to have to tell Dad, we might have an epidemic on our hands. A part of me didn't want to tell Dad, mice were so cute, they didn't deserve to die in a mouse trap, but they can't be stealing my nuts also. I curled up back in bed, thinking of the poor mice my Dad was going to be exterminating in the days to come and contemplated not telling him. I started thinking about my situation. I had the light of a goddess in my body. It all felt unreal. According to Hayden it was all very real and it was very real that people wanted to exterminate me. Then a thought came to me... how did a mouse get inside my jewellery box with the lid shut!

Hayden sat down on my bed and knuckle rubbed my hair.

"Hayden!" I moaned.

"Wake up sleepyhead," he whispered into my ear.

"Hayden, you're so annoying!" He laughed and I caved. "Alright, I'm awake now." I sat up and pushed my pillow up against my bedhead and leaned against it. "What's up?"

"Not you" he joked.

I shoved him "I am now thanks to *someone*."

He pushed my other pillow up against my bedhead and leaned against it beside me. "What do you want to do today?"

I thought about it, I didn't really want to do anything. "Nothing, let's just relax. Spend the day at home."

He put his arms up behind his head and took a deep breath. "That sounds like a great plan. Perfect."

Tom poked his head in the door "Hey Hayden."

"Hey Tom" Hayden replied.

Tom took off down the hallway to his bedroom. I heard his door slam shut.

I smiled. Tom really liked Hayden. He was probably checking to see what we were up to and to see if he could steel Hayden away from me for a game on his PlayStation.

Hayden turned to me. "I'll play him later. This time I'll beat him."

I smiled at him.

"What? I will, I totally will do it this time."

"Whatever." I said as I sunk deeper into bed and pulled the comforter up over us both. "Hayden, how old are you?"

He looked at me "old?"

"Yeah, how old? You're my protector, *apparently*, so that must mean that you've either lived for a very long time, or you're the same age as me and when you were born you became my protector, just like I'm part goddess. I'm just trying to figure this all out."

He sighed. "I'm a lot older than you."

"I knew it, how old?"

"Very old."

I looked at him "Like thousands of years old?" He nodded his head. "So you've just been wandering this earth looking for me?"

"Well kind of like that, but not wandering this earth, I've been wandering multiple worlds looking and searching for the light of Brigid. It's been my sole purpose for many years, so many in fact I can't remember a time in my existence that I thought about anything else."

I gave him a cheeky smile. "Hayden… are you obsessed with me?" I joked.

"Something like that" he smirked.

"There's so much I want to ask you, but there's so many it's all jumbled up."

"Spit it out, the first one that comes to your mind."

"Are you lonely?"

He looked shocked. "Lonely?"

I'm guessing by his expression that he didn't expect that to be my first question. "Yes lonely. You've been alive for thousands of years looking for the light of Brigid. What about you? What about your life? What about a family or a girlfriend?"

He looked sad and pretended to pick his nails. I think I struck a nerve. "Yes I suppose it's been a bit lonely, but you wouldn't understand the importance of you. You need to be kept safe, kept here and live out your life."

"Well, what happens when I grow old and die, do you then go in search for the next one? Does my light just move to the next person? Do you grow old? People would wonder if you didn't grow old with me."

He held his hands up "Whoa, slow down. Yes, I'll always be searching for the light of Brigid, and I'll grow old, kind of. I'll glammer myself to look old and age appropriately with you."

"You can do that?"

He nodded. Wow, that's pretty cool.

"Will you be sad?"

"Sad?"

"When I grow old and die?"

He hugged me and I felt happier in his arms. "Of course I'll be sad. The light drew me to you, but there's something about you as a human that is unforgettable."

I smiled as he hugged me tighter. I wiped my tongue over my teeth. Yeow, I had morning fuzzies. I pulled away from him and walked to my ensuite bathroom to brush my teeth. "Where do you live?" I asked with a mouthful of toothpaste.

"Duh, where do you think Brig...? Dunedin" he replied implying that I was stupid.

"No, I don't mean now, but where are you from? Where do you call home?"

It was silent for a long time. I spat out my toothpaste and rinsed my toothbrush under the tap waiting for an answer. "It's hard to say where I call home. I suppose it will be where I spent my time with Brigid in the Otherworld. But I have lived everywhere, in Ireland, Wales, Scotland, Britain, China, New Zealand – everywhere, but the Otherworld is probably the one I'd call home."

The Otherworld, I'll have to google that place later and learn more about it. "Is that where the gods live?"

"Yeah I suppose, there're different realms in the Otherworld, entirely different places than each other. It's a huge place, but a lot of them call earth their home too."

"Hmm, sounds interesting. Is this where Brigid is? I mean the frozen Brigid."

I sat down at the end of the bed and wiped the rest of the water off my face. "Yes." That's all he said. I left it at that. I got the feeling I'd asked too many questions as it was. I'll ask more another time, but for now I was hungry.

"Morning Brig" Dad called as he poked his balding head through my bedroom door. He looked at my bed, "hey Hayden" he said suspiciously.

"Hey Mr Ports" Hayden replied back with a nod of his head.

Dad squared his eyes on me. "Hayden hasn't been here all night has he?"

"No!" I blurted out. I looked at Hayden tucked under the comforter in my bed and saw why he might think that. "No, not at all."

"Mrs Ports let me in before" Hayden blurted out as he looked at me and winked.

My face was going red. How embarrassing, Dad thought Hayden and I were boyfriend and girlfriend. That couldn't be further than the truth. He was my best friend, my buddy.

"Good" Dad said simply as he started to disappear down the stairs.

"Hey Dad!" I yelled out after him.

"Yeah!" he replied back. His steps slowed to a stop.

"I think we have mice again?"

I heard him mumble swearwords to himself before he answered me. "Okay thanks, I'll look into it."

"Cool thanks, in my bedroom I think that's where they're hanging out." I thought back to the nut crumbs. I felt sorry for the poor mice, but it was either them or my food and I was a hungry girl.

I stood up off the bed. "He is so embarrassing" I said to Hayden. "Sorry about that."

"Nah don't be sorry, at least he cares."

"Yeah, true." I replied. "Right lets go downstairs and get some breakfast. I. am. Starving."

"Right on Brig - I. am. Starving too", Hayden mimicked. I laughed at him as we swerved our way down the stairs, play punching each other on our arms.

CHAPTER 9

We hadn't done much all day, as we promised ourselves in my bed that morning. We went downstairs, had breakfast and a couple of cups of coffee to rinse it down with. Hayden played a couple of games of PlayStation with Tom, and yes Tom bet him... again. I still had my pyjamas on, I hadn't changed all day. It was great having a lazy day. I think we rubbed off on everyone else in the house, because Mum decided to order pizza for tea. Then we all sat down and watched a movie. Hayden left about 10 o'clock. Tom was already in bed, and that's where I was heading. I said goodnight to my parents and made my way up the stairs.

I decided to jump into the shower before I climbed into bed, since the only thing I've cleaned all day was my teeth. I closed my eyes as the warm water tumbled against my skin. I turned the heat up a bit more and hung my head as the water massaged my neck. Oh that felt good. I closed my eyes and thought about the man in my dreams - Cichol. I was so annoyed with him. I know he was just from my dreams, but I'd actually met him and he wanted to kill me. It was crazy. I just didn't believe it. He seemed so sincere and I had trusted him. For some reason I had completely trusted him. I just couldn't imagine that he would have killed me if I'd stayed any longer with him. Hayden had said that he'd do and say anything to me. He wanted my trust. Who was I to second guess him? Hayden had lived for years, and been looking for me for years to protect me from people like him. I sighed, because for some reason I still loved him. Oh my god, did I just think that? No, not love him, I didn't even know him. I meant liked him, trusted him. I trusted him, had trusted him and I'm finding it hard to believe he's evil.

I jumped out of the shower and grabbed the towel to dry myself. Once I'd wrapped the towel around my wet hair, I went to wipe the condensation off the mirror to look at my face and my heart stopped. On the mirror was a "stick figure" picture of a man with sharp pointy teeth. It was a crude picture at best, and his hands were held up like claws. I took a step back and looked again. What? I looked again. What is this? Was this meant to scare me? Who would have done this? Hayden? No, Hayden wouldn't do this, he was supposed to keep me safe. Tom? It must've been Tom. He was the culprit I knew it. I put my pyjamas on and ran downstairs. Mum and Dad were still watching TV.

"Mum, Dad!" I said loudly as I came belting down the stairs two at a time nearly tripping over Winkles our cat at the bottom.

"Yes Brig" Dad replied as he looked up at me when I got into the lounge.

"Come and have a look and see what Tom has done to my mirror."

"Oh Brig, what's he done now?" Mum asked with a huff. She looked tired and ready for bed.

"Just come and look." I said frantically. I needed my parents to see this so Tom could be dealt with in the morning. He can't just go around doing stuff like that in my bedroom. My bedroom was my sanctuary, not a place for my little brother's pranks.

Dad got off his chair and followed me. Mum reluctantly followed behind.

"Look" I whined as I walked into the bathroom.

"Look at what?" Mum asked as she wiped at her tired eyes.

I looked at the mirror, it was gone. The whole mirror had been wiped. There was no condensation left on it. The picture was gone.

"What? I swear that there was a picture of a man with sharp pointy teeth drawn on that mirror. Not drawn with felts but... look when I had a shower and the condensation got on the mirror the scary picture showed up."

"Right" Dad said.

"You believe me right?"

"Brig, we do, we do believe you. Let us know if it happens again okay."

I looked at the mirror again and sighed. "Okay." They didn't believe me, I could tell. Maybe it was my imagination. There was some crazy stuff going on in my life at the moment, who knows my eyes might have made the image up in my mind. I was starting to doubt myself. I felt like Alice in Wonderland.

Mum gave me a hug before they both said goodnight and locked up the house for the night.

The picture on the mirror disturbed me. Why would Tom do this? The more I thought about it the more I thought it wasn't him. He was a pain, but I don't think he'd do that. I'd ask in the morning to confirm it. If I looked him in the eyes and asked him, no matter what his answer was I'd know if he was lying or not.

I tucked myself up in bed and opened my book. I felt warm from my shower and warm with my duvet tucked tightly around me. I was still slightly freaked out though. I closed my eyes and took a deep breath to relax myself then started reading my book. I got a couple of chapters in when…

Crunch, crunch, crunch…

It was that mouse again! I heard it again. I stopped my breathing to see if I could hear it again. Nothing, it had stopped. I'm going to find that mouse and toss it out of the house. I was now on a mission to find it and move it out of my bedroom. I sneakily swung my legs over my bed and sat up slowly, as not to give myself a way to the mouse. I tiptoed to my desk and kept still, listening - still nothing. I was sure I heard it before. I slowly opened up my jewellery box, nothing just my trinkets but the crumbs were gone. This mouse was becoming annoying. I'll remind Dad in the morning about it. I lifted up the jewellery box and turned it in my hands. How was the mouse getting in there anyway? There's no way a mouse could lift the lid and there were no visible holes that I could see that they could get through. I went slowly down to the kitchen and opened the pantry door in search of some flour. I put some in a cup and made my way back up the stairs to my room. I sprinkled some flour over my study desk and some on the shelves. I was going to find out what this mouse was getting up to and how it was getting into my jewellery box. I gently put the jewellery box back on the top shelf and slid quietly into bed and waited.

I woke up to the sun shining through the crack in my curtains. I'd dreamt of my dream man again last night. The dream man that wanted me dead. He was pleading with me to come back to save them. I really wanted to save him. Why did I feel this way about him, it agitated me? I knew there was nothing to save, Brigid the Goddess was frozen, yes, but everyone was happy according to Hayden. I sat up quickly and remembered about that blasted mouse - Argh, I must've fallen asleep. I was hoping to catch me a mouse. Then I remembered the flour. I threw the blankets off and jumped out of bed. Low and behold, it had worked. I started to get excited and clapped my hands as I jumped up and down – yes! There were little footprints all over the study desk. I looked closer. What? I looked again, that's strange, I don't think these are mouse foot prints, they looked like little shoe prints. I shook my head as I closed my eyes. Maybe I was seeing things. They definitely were little shoe marks. I looked up on the shelves, the same thing, lots of random shoe marks and little hand prints. I grabbed the jewellery box and opened it up. What was going on? There was flour everywhere, over all my trinkets and up the sides of the pink velvet cloth that lined the inside of the box. I looked closer and a pair of floured footprints moved. My heart stopped. I kept still and kept my eyes on the flour. No more movement happened. I shook it gently up and down, nothing. I was sure it had moved before. I threw the jewellery box back on the top shelf and ran down the stairs. My heart was thumping and I was too scared to go back up into my room. Whatever was up there, it certainly wasn't a mouse.

"Hey Brig" Tom said as he wandered into the kitchen rubbing his eyes. His brown curly hair was everywhere. He needed a haircut. Tom was two years younger than me and just about as tall.

I was drinking my second cup of coffee for the morning, I was freaking out. "Hey" I replied. Then I remembered about the bathroom mirror. "Were you in my room yesterday by any chance?"

"Yeah, remember I grabbed your phone charger for you when you were watching movies with Hayden in your pyjamas, seriously Brig, did you even get changed yesterday?"

"No actually I didn't." I smiled sneakily at him, yesterday was an excellent lazy day. "When you were up there, did you do anything else?"

"No."

"Really?"

"No, I did nothing else while I was up there. I grabbed your charger and brought it downstairs for you like you asked. Jeez, if this is the response I'm gonna get when I help you, don't bother asking next time." He had his *cat bum* face on. The Cat bum face was what I called his face when he screwed it up and his mouth turned into a cats bum - grumpy hormonal teenager.

I held his eye contact the whole time he replied. He was telling the truth. His face started to go red when he was lying and his eyes would dart around the room, avoiding eye contact at all costs. The sharp toothed drawing of that man on my bathroom mirror wasn't Tom, maybe it was Hayden after all… but why would he do that? "No reason." I told him. I decided to leave it at that and not push the matter. "Thanks for getting my charger though."

"Whatever," Tom replied as he pushed passed me to the pantry.

I wanted to get down to the bottom of things. I grabbed Mum's laptop and sat down at the kitchen table and yes I was still in my Pyjamas. There was no way I was going back up into my room to get changed when I had something running around up there. I started it up and went straight to Google. First thing I looked up was the Otherworld. I wanted to know where Hayden was from. There wasn't a lot about the Otherworld on Google, but what I did get was that in the Otherworld there's believed to be layers of existence of supernatural beings and spirits. It didn't really go into it, but I guess it would mean that they somehow live on top of each other in different parallel realms? That's what I could understand from the Google search. These "realms" can generally be reached by a tree, river, rope or something that represented an imaginary line. I don't think Google knew much about it or anyone did for that matter, but all cultures believed in the Otherworld in some form or another. It was like Kate said at practice the other day – *myths normally start with some sort of truth*, or something like that.

Now, on to the most pressing matter… the footprints on top of my study desk. I know that a mouse did not make those prints, but what did? A shiver crawled up my spine. Whatever it was had little shoes and very little hands. That's the first thing I Googled – *What would wear little shoes?* All google came up with was "Orthopedic" problems. Okay, so clearly I was going to have to think outside the square. Next I typed - *pests with little hands and feet.* This came up with types of bed bugs and bug bites, those definitely weren't right otherwise I'd be itching all over. How was I to explain to Google what I needed to know? Right, I thought to myself, I know this is crazy but I typed it anyway – *mythical little creatures.* Bingo, I think this was more like it, or was it? Maybe the light in my body was making my mind think of crazy things or beings that did not exist, but there were little hand marks on my shelves, now I'm no insect/mammal expert but I have never seen these marks before and with all that's gone on in my life this past week, could it really be that unbelievable? The first creature that came up was an "Adaro" – I'd never heard of it before and I don't think this fitted the description anyway. They are half human and half fish, and aggressive little fish by the sounds of it, attacking humans with flying fish – weird. The next one below it was "Brownies." Brownies were invisible brown elves or house goblins that lived in Scottish houses and did favours for the household owner while they slept and by the sounds of it they were loyal creatures and protective of the families they chose to live with, but if they were treated badly they disappeared, vanished. A payment of something to eat is given to the brownies by the Scottish people for the favours they would do for them. The next one was "Gremlins." I cringed, I'd seen the movie Gremlins and I definitely don't think we have one of those in the house, or it would have turned to turmoil by now and besides the footprints were too small to be a gremlin, according to the size they were in the movie anyway. I skipped to the next ones, "Leprechauns" and "Pixies" were next up. Leprechauns apparently help people like Brownies in exchange for food, Pixies were thought to have not been good enough to go into Heaven and not bad enough to go to Hell and were doomed to walk the earth forever. They were tricksters but hardworking. I shut the screen to Mum's laptop. I don't think Google helped. There's no way I have a Brownie, Leprechaun or Pixie in my house, that wasn't plausible, but what was it? Whatever it was, I had to catch it, and I had to know what the hell it was. I started to think back about giving them food in return for favours. This seemed to be the common theme, but what to leave? Once again I turned to Google and decided on cream. I was going to leave a bowl of cream in my room and I was going to be hiding to catch it in action. I smiled as I thought about how sneaky I was, then the smile disappeared as I realised I was going to have to go into my room again to set it up.

I had my eyes on the bowl of cream that I'd put on my study desk. I tucked myself under my blankets with my torch light. I was going to catch this thing if it was the last thing I did. My eyes started to get tired. I grabbed my book and read it under my blankets for a while with the torch lighting the pages. Then I started to hear it, the slurping from the cream bowl. My heart nearly leapt out of my chest – yes! It was faint, but it was definitely a slurping sound. I slowly lifted the duvet off me and shone the torch quickly on the cream bowl so I could catch it in action.

I screamed and dropped the torch on the floor. The little man with his butt crack showing knocked over the bowl of cream and disappeared in front of my eyes. I threw the duvet over me again and tried to reach down to get my torch. OMG, there was a little man in my house, in my room! Google was right! I could hear my heart pumping in my chest and a whirring noise in my ears. Get it together Brigid, I said to myself, you have the light of a goddess running through your veins, you can deal with this. I reached down lower and felt along the floor. My hand scraped against the torch and I grabbed it. I slowly threw the duvet off me and sat up at the side of my bed. I shone the torch again to my study desk. There was a puddle of cream and footprints leading up to my jewellery box. I took a deep breath in, you can do this Brigid. I sat up and walked slowly over to my jewellery box. I quickly opened it and shone the torch in. Nothing, only splatters of cream against the pink velvet lining.

"Hello" I whispered. I waited for a while and said it again when I got no reply.

"Hello. My name is Brigid, I won't hurt you. Hopefully you won't hurt me." I heard a scuffle and saw some of my trinkets move. I knew it was in there. It *was* a mythical creature after all, it must be because what else would be invisible.

"I saw you before. Its okay, I'm friendly… do you want some more cream? I'm sorry I frightened you and made you spill it." It was still quiet in my jewellery box, but I knew it could hear me and it was listening.

"I'll tell you what. I'll go and get you the biggest bowl of cream if you show yourself to me."

I waited for a good couple of minutes. "I promise I won't hurt you, I just want to see you and I really want to give you a big bowl of cream. You seemed to be really enjoying it before I rudely interrupted before."

I waited a while longer. I didn't think it was going to show itself. I huffed, this wasn't helping. I didn't want to sleep in my room with some creature I didn't know. I didn't know if it wanted to harm me or not. I slowly put the box back up on the shelf. I went to shut the lid when I saw a couple of large pointy ears. It stood up and smiled at me. It had cream all over its face. My heart melted, it looked so cute! How could this cute little creature want to harm me? It moved backwards to the far corner of the box, looking warily at me. This thing wasn't going to hurt me, I knew it in my bones.

"I won't hurt you, I just wanted to know what you were and who you were."

He went to talk but nothing came out. His hand went up to his neck and he nodded his little head. He was wearing a little brown woollen cap with huge pointy ears poking out of it. He had on raggedy brown clothes with little brown boots. His large black eyes were wide apart and nearly sat on the side of his face. He was so ugly that he was cute.

"Can you not talk?" I asked as I held my own throat, mimicking him in case he couldn't understand me.

He nodded his head sadly.

"Can you understand me?"

He nodded again as he scratched his bum. He smiled and I saw a row of pointy little teeth which was slightly worrying.

"Are you going to hurt me?" I asked him.

He threw his head back and opened his mouth. He held his round belly as he shook. He was laughing. I smiled at his reaction. He stopped laughing and shook his head. He pulled his pants up further and rocked back and forth.

"That's good" I said delighted he wasn't going to hurt me. I think at the back of my mind I already knew that. "What are you? Sorry I know you can't answer that, how about I ask you a question and you can nod or shake your head to answer me – okay?"

He nodded his little head again.

"Okay, so are you a pixie?"

He screwed up his huge nose in disgust. "Okay so you're not a Pixie."

He shook his head roughly.

"Are you a brownie?"

He nodded with his eyes wide and a huge smile beaming on his face.

"Wow! You're a brownie?"

He kept nodding his head, but stayed to the back corner of the box.

"Why are you here? I mean, why are you living in my room?"

He shrugged his shoulders and looked confused.

"You don't know?"

He shrugged his shoulders again. He held his finger up and looked at me. He then pushed his arms up over his head in a circular motion and then looked at me again to see if I understood what he was trying to tell me. He was about as big as my index finger, he was so tiny.

I had no idea what he was trying to explain. I shrugged my shoulders. "Sorry, I don't understand."

He tapped his little foot in frustration, and then held his finger up for my attention. He pushed his arms up over his head again in a circular motion then froze looking up at the roof. He paused there for a moment for effect before he looked at me again.

"Sorry, I still don't understand."

He looked like he was growling with frustration. He climbed out of the jewellery box and dropped to the shelf below it. He climbed down that one and dropped to my study desk onto the spilt cream. He put his finger in the cream and started to draw a picture. He started with a circle with lots of little lines poking out from it. When he was satisfied with what he'd drawn, he licked the cream off his fingers.

"It's a sun!" I yelled. Then held my hands over my lips when I realised I could have just woken up my whole family. "Sorry, I meant – is it a sun?"

He smiled and nodded his head.

"You are here because of the sun?"

He nodded again and drew a stick figure of a girl with long hair beside the sun. Then it dawned on me.

"You are here because of Brigid, the sun goddess."

He put his hands on his hips and smiled broadly. He pulled out a little sword from the back of his pants and swung it around pretending to fight someone.

I jumped back a bit, I did not expect that. It didn't seem like he wanted to hurt me though, he was showing me something. It looked like he was protecting me from something.

"Are you protecting me?"

He put his sword away and bowed.

"Well thank you, I certainly appreciate it." It was nice to think he was here to protect me. "I already have a protector though."

He looked at me and shook his head as he screwed up his large nose again. His large pointy ears wiggled with the movement. I really wished he could talk to me. It would make this so much easier. He kept shaking it and held up his finger for my attention. I nodded my head to show him I was paying attention. He drew a picture of a man with sharp pointy teeth and then put a big cross through it. He looked up at me for my reaction.

I didn't understand, but I think I just found the culprit of the picture in my mirror. "Did you draw that picture on my mirror?"

He nodded his head and bared his teeth. He wrapped his little arms around himself and turned so his back was showing to me. His hands were clutching his back. He started rubbing them up and down. He then turned his head and puckered his lips like he was kissing someone. He jumped back around to face me again and bared his sharp pointy teeth.

I shook my head, "I'm sorry I don't understand?" Gosh he was cute.

He threw his hands up in frustration and sat down on the edge of the desk with his hands on his head.

It upset me to see him so frustrated, but I didn't know what he was trying to say. I decided to change the subject. We can try and work this out another time. "I promised you something didn't I?"

He looked up at me with his wide black eyes with a look of anticipation.

"Does somebody want some cream?"

He jumped up and nodded his head licking his lips.

"Okay, I'll go downstairs and get some more. Do you like my jewellery box?" I asked him.

He nodded and put his hands together and put them both to the side of his face and pretended to sleep.

I laughed at his cute interpretation. "Okay, you can sleep there if you want." I smiled "I'll be right back".

How cute, I'll have a brownie sleeping in my room, that's a bit different from the norm. I don't think any other teenager in New Zealand can say the same.

I came back up with a big bowl of cream and some cotton balls. I gave the bowl of cream to the Brownie. He jumped up and down and ran to the bowl. He bent over and started to slurp. I laughed at him as his bum crack appeared again when he bent over. I leant over and gently pulled them up slightly. He stopped slurping and looked up at me as he wiped his mouth. He nodded his head in thanks and gave me a cheeky smile, I was sure he was laughing. I then put the cotton balls in the jewellery box and organised them so they were a comfortable mattress.

"There that will be better" I said to him.

He ignored me as he slurped at the cream. I went to my drawers and grabbed out a bandana from my underwear drawer. This will do for a blanket for him. Hopefully he'll be warm enough I thought to myself. It was summer, so he shouldn't need too many blankets. It was still hot at night, but if he was staying with me over the winter, I'll organise something else to keep him warm from the cold Dunedin nights.

Once he finished his cream I held my hand out for him to climb onto it. He looked at me with a confused look on his face. "Well, it's better than climbing up those shelves." I told him.

He nodded and walked onto my hand. He was heavier than he looked. I gently placed him in the box. I went to close the lid. "Good night Brownie." He smiled at me as I smiled back. I shut the lid and climbed into bed. I had a Brownie in my house, what a turn of events.

CHAPTER 10

The Brownie quickly made himself at home, he was quite adorable. One night, I caught him stealing Burger Rings from my brother while he was playing his video games in the lounge. When he realised I'd caught him, he gave me the cheekiest smile with chip crumbs spilling out of his overfilled mouth and disappeared. He took great delight in riding the cat, Winkles, up and down the stairs. Winkles, believe it or not, didn't seem to mind, she took it in her stride. The Brownie would grab Winkles's long ginger fur with one hand and hold the other one up in the air as Winkles bounded up and down the stairs, like he was riding a bull at a rodeo. His large pointy ears bounced in delight as he threw his head back showing his spikey teeth in silent laughter. The rest of my family just thought Winkles was going mad with age, they couldn't see the Brownie riding it like a bull as it bounded up and down the stairs. He even fixed my Dad's shelf in the garage and the sensor light outside. My Dad was absolutely amazed. He spent the next few days trying to figure out who'd done it. He knew me, Mum or Tom wouldn't have fixed it. My Mum and I had no idea about DIY and Tom, well let's just say Tom was too lazy to fix anything. I asked the Brownie if he'd fixed them, he smiled and nodded his head looking chuffed with himself. I thanked him and gave him a bowl of cream which he slurped away at eagerly. So that's what happened every night, it became a routine. I'd leave a bowl of cream, or nuts, or anything that I knew he liked on my study desk before I went to sleep at night. It didn't take me long to realise that the Brownie was nocturnal. He slept during most of the day and was awake at night. Some nights I'd wake up to him gently pulling my eyelids open trying to wake me up for a game of draughts. He loved that game. I learnt to love him. He was so much fun and cheeky and the cat loved him too. Winkles spent more time in my room than she'd ever done in the past. He did odd jobs around the house, he was a delight and extremely helpful. I just wished I could tell my family about him, but they didn't seem to be able to see him and that was his choice. I knew that he didn't want them to see him. One day maybe he'd trust them. I knew deep in my heart that they would accept him, especially when he used his magic to wash the dishes that were left out at night, that I was currently taking the credit for in the mornings. They would love him and when the time was right I was sure he'd show himself to them.

I jumped out of the shower in a rush. Hayden was coming to pick me up, it was Friday and we were going to a bomb-fire party out at Stephen's house in East Taieri. It was going to be huge! It had become sort of a ritual in Dunedin for our school and Stephen had been doing it for the last few years. Mum had even brought me a four-pack of Bacardi Breezer RTDs to take with me this year. I reassured her that Hayden would drop me back at home by 10.30pm and no later. I had tried for 11.00pm, but my Dad wasn't having a bar of it. I flicked my wet hair forward and wrapped my grey towel around it. I twisted the length of it and then stood up as I flicked it down my back and looked at myself in the mirror. Staring back at me was another picture. This time it was a stick figure picture of a girl with long hair holding a little stick figure in her hand with big pointy ears. There was a smile on the little stick figure's circle face. I broke into a smile. It was a picture of my little Brownie and me. He was showing me that we were friends. He was such a little dude. I had to find a name for him… calling him

Brownie wasn't right. A thought popped into my head. What about "B?" It could be short for Brownie. I reckoned it would be okay for now. I made a mental note to ask him when I saw him later that night. I looked at my watch. It was going on 7.00pm, Hayden would be here soon. He was picking me up at 7.30pm. I took one last look at my awesome picture B drew for me and walked eagerly out of my bathroom to figure out what I was going to wear. We would be out on a farm, so I thought faded blue denim jeans and maybe a loose black high low top would work. I'd definitely be wearing my brown boots his time. I remembered Stephen's bomb fire party from last year and the amount of cow and sheep poo I had on the bottom of my feet was disgusting! They smelt for days. I would not be wearing sandals to Stephen's farm again in a hurry.

I heard the doorbell ring downstairs. Hayden was here, I took one last look at myself, satisfied that I looked okay and grabbed my hand bag as I made my way to the stairs. I lifted my bag up as I felt something moving inside. I opened it up. B!

"B, what are you doing in there?" I asked him. He looked up at me with a questioning look. "Oh, I thought I could call you B from now on, just until you can tell me what your real name is? Are you okay with that?"

He thought about it for a while and gave me a thumbs up and winked at me. I smiled and kissed him on the forehead. He blushed as he sat back down in the bag and started to do up the zip.

"Whoa" I said as I stopped him. "You can't come with me."

He nodded his head and put his hands on his little hips in a defiance stanch.

Dam, this wasn't going to be easy breaking it to him. "B, you can't come with me. There'll be lots of people there, and well, you would probably find it boring." He didn't look convinced. "It could be dangerous for you." With that last comment he puffed out his chest and withdrew his sword from the back of his pants. He pointed it at me and then to himself pouting his lips.

"I get it, you want to protect me, but I'll be perfectly safe, I'll be with Hayden and Kate."

He bared his pointy teeth and swung his sword around vigorously.

"What? Why are you getting so angry?"

He crossed his arms and turned his back to me.

My heart melted what trouble would it be to take him. He could just stay in my handbag I convinced myself. No one would see him unless he wanted them to anyway. "Okay" I huffed.

He jumped around and clapped his hands.

"Yeah, no need to pee your pants about it" I laughed. "You need to promise me you'll stay in my handbag. I need to make sure you're safe. I'd hate for someone to stand on you and squish you."

He crossed his little heart with his index finger and a luminescent light of a cross shone in the air by his heart before it faded away. He was a clever wee thing. I had a feeling there were things about B that I was yet to find out about.

"Looking good Brig" Hayden said as I climbed into his car.

"Thanks, so do you." I said to him truthfully. He did look good, he had on faded blue jeans too and his black faded Nirvana t-shirt on. "You actually managed to do your hair this time." I joked.

He rubbed my hair and messed it up in response. "Smarty pants."

We picked up Kate on the way. She looked really cute. She had on a yellow summer skater dress which reached mid-thigh and black ankle boots.

"Heya Kate" I said as she climbed into the backseat.

"Hey guys!" she said over excited. "Wow, you both look very fresh. Do you think I dressed up too much?"

Hayden and I both looked at each other. "No way" we said in unison with smiles on our faces. Maybe she'd forgotten we are going to a farm.

"Come on guys, be truthful… do you think I've over-done it?"

"No not at all Kate, you look beautiful" I reassured her. "I think I could have tried a bit harder actually."

"Are you hoping a certain someone is there tonight?" Hayden asked Kate as he readjusted his rear vision mirror.

"Of course! Why else would I go to such an effort" she scoffed.

We all laughed. "Well Kate, you pulled it off and I'm sure Holden will be there tonight." Holden was the crush Kate currently had. Actually she'd had a crush on him for years, it wasn't a new thing. Holden was a jock, a sporty guy. His favourite sport being Rugby like every young New Zealand male and he looked every bit of a rugby head too, messy dirty blond hair, stocky build, always in shorts or track pants. Kate was his polar opposite, but she liked him and he seemed to have taken a recent interest in her too.

We pulled up to the party. There were loads of people there as I expected. We soon found our normal crew of people and sat down on the hay bales beside them. I could feel the warmth of the bomb fire that was in the middle of the party, surrounded by lots of hay bales and even more people. I cracked open one of my Bacardi Breezers and took a sip. The sweet taste slid down my throat, it tasted good. I gave one to Kate to drink and we sat there relishing in its sweetness and the heat of the fire. I'd gently put my hand bag on my lap as I crossed my legs making sure I hadn't zipped it all the way up so B could breathe. That would be horrible… death by handbag suffocation.

Kate had gone off with Holden and I was with Hayden sipping on my last Bacardi Breezer standing by the bomb fire.

"I love looking at fire" I said to Hayden. "I love the movements of the flames, it looks like they're alive. I could look at it for hours." I felt like I was in a trance, the flames had me captivated.

He looked at me. "Maybe you need some water?"

"Hayden, I don't need water. I've only had two drinks, I'm fine."

"Regardless, I'll get you some water anyway. I'll be back soon."

Hayden left in the search for some water. I kept my eyes on the fire taking in its warmth and watching each individual flame dance. I could feel my arm starting to tingle and instinctively I put my cardigan on and pulled down the sleeves. I knew what that meant. I lifted my handbag up onto my shoulder as I ditched my empty Bacardi Breezer in the old steel bin. I checked in on B. He gave me the thumbs up but motioned for me to leave the zip undone, so I did.

"Here" Hayden said as he handed me a red plastic cup fill of water.

"Thanks." I took a big gulp, he was right, I did need this water, and my throat was so dry from standing by the fire for so long.

"Don't mention it."

We both stood there in silence as people walked back and forth talking and laughing. I could feel my arm. I knew without even looking at it that it was glowing. There was something about this party and this fire that had my goddess blood inside of me all in a tiss. I looked down at my water. A ripple ran through it. I swished it around and watched the ripples hit the side of the cup.

"*Brigid*" a quiet whisper filled my ears. I'd heard that voice before at Cargill's Castle, whispering to me as I'd walked away. I looked back down at my water with wide eyes. Maybe Hayden was right, maybe those two drinks had gone straight to my head. There was a woman looking back at me from my cup of water. Her long copper hair was moving gracefully with the ripples, she had the most intense green eyes. I nearly dropped my cup.

"*Brigid*" She whispered again. I turned to Hayden to see if he could hear her. He was looking into the fire, so I assumed he couldn't.

"*Brigid… come to me.*"

"What?" I whispered into my cup. "Are you talking to me?"

"*Yes, you are our saviour - come to me. Come through the oak trees.*" She looked sad, she was absolutely beautiful. The most beautiful person I'd ever seen. Her copper hair swished back and forth over her delicate face.

I didn't know whether to trust her or not, I wanted to, but was this another trick by Cichol? I wasn't sure. "Are you real?" I asked.

"*Yes Brigid, I am very real, you must come, you must save us, you…*"

She stopped mid-sentence and disappeared as the flames in the bomb fire burst into a higher flame and the sound of something lightly exploding filled my ears. "You what? What?" I desperately asked my cup of water.

I could hear Hayden chanting, whispering words I didn't recognise. He opened his eyes and put his hand on my shoulder. "Are you okay?"

"Yeah I guess. What were you whispering?" He had obviously been aware of the voice in my cup of water. He must've had his protector ears on.

"A spell to get rid of the negative spirit that appeared *uninvited* in your water… Pretty rude if you ask me." A smile broke on his face, trying to make light of the situation, but concern was on face. He was worried.

"Do you think that was the guy from my dreams again trying to trick me?"

"The one and only" he replied. He took his wooden beaded bracelet off of his wrist. He brought it up to his lips and covered it with his hands. He closed his eyes and murmured something under his breath as he breathed into his hands. He held it out to me. "Here wear this. This will stop any uninvited guests making an appearance again."

I took the bracelet off him and put it on around my wrist. If this was going to keep me safe, I was all for it. I felt the soft wood against my skin. "Your lip's bleeding!"

"Yeah, I had to invoke the spell with blood. Don't worry it'll heal." I must've looked worried because he pulled me into a hug. "The things I do for you Brigid Ports."

I pulled away from him as I felt my bag moving. B's head popped out over the top of the zip. I motioned for him to hide. He waved his hands in front of his face and shook his head. Of course, he was invisible to other people except for me. I mouthed "Okay" to him. He nodded and looked to Hayden who had his back turned to us while he talked to Levi from our maths class. B bared his teeth and put his hands up like claws. He pointed to Hayden. I shook my head at him. B pointed again desperately trying to get me to understand him. I tried to act natural as a group of girls walked past. They couldn't see B but they could see me. B was beside himself now. He'd drawn his little sword and was getting ready to jump on Hayden's back.

"No!" I yelled as I grabbed B before he hit his mark.

Hayden spun around as I shoved B back in my bag and zipped it up. "What?"

"Nothing, I thought I'd stood on cow poo, but nope, I haven't." I pretended to inspect my foot as I held it up so I could see it better.

He looked at me strangely. "Right… how about we head off now, it's been eventful. Gotta get you home on time or Mr Ports will smack me over the head then dig my grave."

"Yeah you're right. I'll go find Kate."

"She's over there." He pointed to the other side of the fire. Holden had his arm around her waist and she was laughing. I hated to wreck her fun, but we had to go or she'd be in trouble too.

I caught her eye and motioned for her to come over. I pointed to my watch which meant we needed to go. She pouted dramatically as she turned to Holden and kissed him. She waved goodbye to him, but Holden pulled her back and kissed her again. She kicked her leg up as the kiss dragged on. OMG she seriously just popped her leg I thought to myself that was so "Princess Diaries."

I got home with five minutes to spare. Unbelievably no one had waited up for me. I raided the fridge for B and me. He sat on my shoulder and directed me to the food he wanted to eat. Tonight it was honey on top of rice bubbles. For me it was left over pizza. I heated it up in the microwave and headed my way up the stairs. As I reached the top Winkles came running up to me and rubbed against my ankles. "Yes" I whispered "B is with me."

B jumped down onto Winkles back as we all walked into my bedroom.

CHAPTER 11

I woke up with a dry mouth. I needed a drink. I crawled out of bed and made my way down the stairs. Winkles meet me at the bottom and gave my legs a quick rub before running off. I made my way to the kitchen sink and poured myself a glass of water. I took a big gulp. I felt its coldness make its way down to my stomach and I welcomed it. I needed this water. I looked in the sink and there sitting at the bottom was my bracelet, the bracelet that Hayden had given me last night. I looked at my wrist to confirm that it was in deed the same bracelet and it was. It was sitting in a bowl of water in the sink. That's strange. I'd been downstairs with B making food late last night, maybe I'd taken it off or it had fallen off? Who knew? I took it out of the water and gave it shake before I sat it on top of a tea towel to dry it off. It smelt salty, must have been some salt in that water. No harm done. It was wood, it would survive.

That night I was so tired when I went to bed. I quickly checked on B to make sure he was okay, then tucked myself under my duvet and went straight to sleep.

Cichol was standing beside the town's fountain. I was staring back up at him from under the water. Strands of his blond hair dusted the side of his chiselled face as he leaned over to talk to me.

"My lady, you are well?"

"Yes I'm well thank you." Wait, why was I making small talk with him, he wanted to kill me. "No, I'm not talking to you. You want to kill me!"

He frowned at me gently. "No Brigid, that is not correct."

My name on his lips sent shivers down my spine. How did he know? "Hayden says that you want to kill me." I started to cry. Oh my god I was crying. That was next level embarrassing, but I couldn't stop.

"I don't know this Hayden? Who is this man?"

"He's my best friend!" I practically yelled it in his face as I wiped my eyes.

Cichol's voice was still gentle when he spoke next. "Well, I think your friend Hayden may have been misinformed. Brigid they have found you, you are in grave danger. I want to help you and we need you to help us from this terror we all live in."

The water started to ripple. I could feel myself being pulled away from him.

"Wait!" He yelled. "Take my hand, come with me and I will show you. I have brought you here momentarily, but you can't stay here for long. Your body is asleep in your world. Your soul is here with me."

"What?"

"Take my hand before you go back through. I need to show you so you will understand. You can wake up and return to your body whenever you want. You are perfectly safe... even if you think I want to kill you." His face scowled as he said the words kill you *and there was even a hint of sarcasm in his words.*

I thought about it. I wanted to go with him and find out more. To be fair I wanted to be with "him" for longer, even if he would be my downfall.

I held out my hand. He took it and pulled me up through the water of the fountain. It felt like I was being pulled from a painting. I grabbed his neck as my feet fumbled on the ground. He grabbed my waist to steady me. I could feel his hard muscles against mine. I backed away, suddenly very aware of how close I was to him.

"Right, show me. Show me what you're so desperately trying to tell me."

"Look around you Brigid." He said as he spread his arms out around him. He had no top on again, just his green skirt, gold belt and his leather wrist and ankle bands. He had his shield strapped to his back and a sword tucked in his belt. "What do you see?"

"I see that you have no top on again" I muttered under my breath low enough so he couldn't hear me. I followed his hands and looked out into the town. Everything was dull, no colour or life to it. There were wooden framed houses with thatched roofs. Hardened dirt roads lined the houses, but there was no people, no life. The fountain that Cichol had pulled me from was surrounded by risen grey rock. It had a statue of a naked little boy holding the sun in one hand and a fish in the other as it conveniently covered his private parts. "Where is everybody?" I asked.

"They are here, just not in sight. They are scared and hiding."

"Scared of what?"

"Of the darkness, of the Fomorians."

I remembered that name. They were the people that froze Brigid. They were the reason that I had the light in my body. "They're responsible for this?"

"Yes"

"But I thought you were all happy and thriving?" I was stunned. Unless this was a trick. "Wait, Hayden told me that you're the enemy, which means you're responsible for all of this." I started to back away, fully aware now of my situation. Why had I let him pull me through that fountain?

"Happy? No we are certainly not happy. The Fomorians have cast a curse on this realm. The only thing keeping us alive at the moment is your light and I am certainly not responsible for all this, I am trying to keep everybody alive." He looked at the town in disgust and regret.

He moved closer to me. I turned and started to run. I felt his hand close tightly around my arm as he spun me around. "Let me go Cichol!" I screamed.

"What?" He released my arm and backed away from me. "What did you call me?"

"Cichol, I called you Cichol. That's your name isn't it?" I was heavy breathing. I needed to get away. I needed to wake up and go back home.

"No it is not." He looked shocked and confused. "My name is Uar."

I stared at him. Things were starting to get confusing. "Your name is not Cichol?"

"No, I can explain more, but we shouldn't be out in the open like this. Here put this on." He pulled out a large grey cloak from the other side of the fountain and draped it around me, pulling the hood up over my head covering my hair. He held out his hand and I took it. Why was I always taking his hand? This whole situation was getting confusing. His name is not Cichol? He pulled me to the back of one of the houses and opened the back wooden door. It squeaked and strained with the movement. Warmth hit me as we walked into a small room. It had a small bed in the far corner, a fire in the centre of the room with what looked like an iron cauldron hanging in the middle of it bubbling away with some brown chunky soup.

"Where are we?"

"We are at my friend's house. We are safe for now, but not for long. They are always searching."

"Who are always searching? You have some serious explaining to do. Who are you?"

"My name is Uar. I am the youngest son of our great Mother, the Goddess of the Flames."

My mouth dropped open. "You are her son?"

He nodded. "My name is not Cichol. Cichol is a Fomorian. He's the enemy."

"I don't understand. Why would Hayden tell me your name was Cichol?" I was confused. Maybe Hayden just got it wrong and just assumed Cichol was the man from my dreams. He'd told me that everybody here was happy that they didn't need Brigid to become unfrozen. This place certainly was not in a happy place right now, even a blind person could see that.

"Who is this Hayden?" He asked as he offered me a seat on the stool beside the fire.

I sat down. "Hayden is my best friend. He was the one that told me about Brigid and the light." Then I realised. Maybe he was tricking me, and he wanted me to confirm that I had the light in my body so he could kill me.

He must've read my thoughts. "Brigid, I know that you have my Mother's light in you. You held my hand, remember and I saw the glow."

"That was in my dream, how do you know that?"

"It wasn't a dream Brigid, you were here with me."

I shook my head in disbelief. I was actually here in my dreams, it was all real. I held his hand and we walked through the hay. I was in complete bliss when

I was with him. I yearned for him so much it hurt. Maybe that's why I kept grabbing his hand. I trusted him, at least "dream me" trusted him.

"You need to tell me about this Hayden. How long have you known him for?"

I didn't want to tell him anything about him. "I've known him for a long time, he's my friend, that's all you need to know. He's protecting me from the Fomorians. Maybe he got you wrong, but he has my back. I trust him."

He didn't believe me, but I wasn't about to snitch on my friend. I didn't know what this Uar guy was capable of.

I changed the subject. "So, all this can be changed if I bring Brigid back to life?"

"Yes."

"When I bring her back to life, will my life become normal again?"

"Yes."

I frowned at that. That would mean that I wouldn't be able to see him again. There'd be no reason to. "Okay, so how do I do this?"

"We need to get you through the Oak Trees and past the bones of judgement."

"The bones of judgement? Are they those creepy little bones tied up in the trees past the meadow of hay?"

"Yes, they will not allow anyone through that has bad intentions towards Mother. They surround her. If your intentions are not true and pure towards her, they will not let you pass."

"Right, judging bones," it seemed a bit odd, but I'd go with it. *"In my dreams, I'd freeze at that point. I could never get past. The only time I got past was when I was with you. What if I go and they won't let me through?"*

"Do you want to help my Mother?"

"Yes."

"Then they will let you through."

I starred at my dream man. He was so cute. He sat on a stool opposite me. His bare tanned skin glistened with the dancing light of the fire. *"You know Uar, I'm finding this all a bit hard to believe,"* which was true. *"You're the son of Brigid, the lady of the sacred flame, but didn't you go into the sea with your Father? Didn't your older brother start all of this?"*

He looked down at the floor. *"I was dragged to the sea by my father's guards."* A dark cloud covered his face. *"I was imprisoned. He said that my Mother could never have me. She was to lose everything. My older brother Ruadan was on my Father's side. He was a ruthless coward. He followed my Father everywhere, and he would do anything my Father asked of him, even kill my Mother and her family. He took his abuse and craved it. I hated him for it. I did not mourn him when he died. Luchar was my middle brother. He kept to himself. He took the side of my father too, but he was afraid of my father, everyone was. He was not imprisoned like me. He wandered around the bottom of the sea as if nothing had happened. It used to infuriate me, until he freed me."*

"He freed you?"

"Yes, he freed me. When I got back here, it was too late. The realm was in mourning. My Mother was gone. It kills me every day to think that my Mother's last thought was of a son and family's ultimate betrayal. They were people she loved and trusted. She would have felt completely lost and I wasn't there for her. The colour of this world faded along with its people when she was frozen. The Fomorians had taken over and drained any joy and love the land offered and with it came

disease and fear. Only your light can bring my Mother back to me, to us all. I never saw my brother Luchar again."

"Right" I was amped now, this was my destiny, and I was doing this. Damn those Fomorians, I needed to save these people, to save Uar. "Let's do this, let's go. Show me where and how."

"First of all, you need to come here."

"I am here."

"No, you're not really here. You are back in your world. It is only your spirit that is here."

I touched my body to confirm that I was here. "Ah, how do I do that?" I asked.

"Go back to the stone. For some reason it has a portal to our world attached to it. Touch the stone, come through."

"Can I get back through? To my world I mean, can I get back through when I've finished."

He nodded.

"I need a more definite answer than that." Just nodding wasn't going to cut it, and it wasn't even a convincing nod.

"Yes, Mother will be able to get you back."

"Brigid! What if I don't succeed, does that mean I'll never be able to come home?"

He shrugged his shoulders. "That is a possibility, I'm powerful, but not as powerful as my Mother, especially now with my powers being muted with the encasement of my mother."

"*You have powers?*"

"*Yes I am a deity, a demi god. You will have powers too. Have you ever noticed any?*"

I thought about it. "*No, I don't think so.*"

He smiled.

"*Why are you smiling? Do you know something I don't know?*"

"*Next time you are in front of a fire, talk to it.*"

"*Talk to it?*"

"*Yes talk to it, it may dance for you. Or better yet it may talk back.*" *He gave me a cheeky wink.*

I looked at him strangely and felt my face turning red with the memory of his wink and what that may have meant. I turned away from him so he couldn't see my face. I was totally going to try it though. How cool would it be if I had super powers! "*Okay, so let's get down to business,*" *I said once my face calmed down.* "*Tomorrow morning I will go down to the castle and come through. Will you be here waiting for me?*"

"*Always,*" *he replied.*

Of course he would be, I thought dreamily to myself. "*Great, do I need to bring anything?*"

He looked at me strangely.

"*Like do I need to bring my toothbrush or anything?*" *He was still looking at me strangely.* "*What I'm trying to find out is whether I'll be here for a long time and if there's anything I need to bring with me?*"

"No, just bring you and your light. That is all we need. But Brigid, you need to hurry, they have found you."

"Who? The Fomorians?"

"Yes the Fomorians. You have to come here to the Otherworld not just to save us but so you can save yourself." He stood up and took my hand. I felt his warmth tingle up my arm. I took a deep breath. "Brigid, they are trying to kill you, they want you dead. They will stop at nothing, you must come here, come to me so I can protect you and so you can save us."

People really did want me dead? "What about my family? If they know where I am will they kill my family?"

"No, I don't think so. They have searched for you for centuries. They will not waste their time with your family." He put his hand on my knee and gave it a squeeze for reassurance. I desperately wanted to put my hand on top of his, but I held back.

I wasn't sure I believed him, if I was in danger surely my family would be in danger too. I could always get Hayden to look after them while I was away. Yes, that's what I'll do, I'll let Hayden know, if anyone could protect them he could.

"Right, so I guess I'll see you again soon." I was ready to go back to my body now, but I had absolutely no idea how to do it. "So… how do I go back to my body?" I asked Uar.

He smiled as he pulled me to my feet by my hands. He held me against his chest and gently placed his head against my neck and screamed, "Wake Up!"

CHAPTER 12

I sat up. "He just yelled at me!"

I was back in my bed, on top of my blankets. B was lying on the far side of my pillow with his bum up in the air, snoring lightly as the sun started to peek through my curtains. I pulled my duvet up over him to keep him warm and cosy. I made my way to my bathroom and splashed some cold water on my face. He yelled at me. I was certainly awake now!

I silently got dressed into my running outfit. I had a feeling I'd need to be agile when I crossed over to the Otherworld, especially if I was being hunted. A shiver ran up my spine. People actually wanted to kill me, it was so scary. I had to get to Brigid and unfreeze her. She'd be the only one, apart from Uar that could save me. I was confused. I should be going to Hayden first and asking him if I was doing the right thing but I had no time to waste. I had to get to Cargill's castle and pass through the portal and get there, for all I knew the Fomorians were on their way to get me now. That made me move faster. I grabbed my small Roxy overnight bag and threw in a clean pair of knickers, a change of clothes, deodorant and of course my toothbrush. I put on some makeup then threw it into my bag, after all – Uar was going to be there, I needed to look my best. Even though I didn't know how I felt about him yet, I still needed to look good. He'd be waiting for me like my knight in shining armour. I sighed, what am I thinking about? Only yesterday I thought he was trying to kill me. Next thing I know, he is the good guy and is there to save my life. Could I trust him? I quietly walked down the stairs so nobody could hear me. I left a note for Mum and Dad, letting them know that I was going to Kate's family's holiday home in Brighton. I'll be back in a couple of days and I'd give them a call. I tucked my phone in my pocket and grabbed Tom's packet of Cheezel's, and a couple of Mum's chocolate bars as I ran out the door. I jumped on my bike and pulled the straps of my bag tighter against my shoulders. It was an overcast day, something was on the horizon, and it had an airy feeling to it. I quickly text Hayden to let him know what I was up to and what was going on. I knew he'd be mad at me for running off like this, but there was no time. He'd keep an eye out on my family. I knew he would.

I pulled up to the small round-about on the top of St Clair Hill. I walked my bike off to the side of the road. Sweat was pouring off me. Biking up those hills was not easy. I gave my eyes a wipe to clear any rouge mascara running down my cheek from my sweaty face. Uar didn't need to see that. The sea was rough this morning I could hear it pounding the bottom of the cliffs below me. Where was I going to put my bike? I decided to walk it to the wire fence and dump it on the ground, hidden in the long grass. Hopefully it'll still be there when I get back. I pulled the wire up and crawled under it. My bag caught on it. I turned around to pull it out when I noticed a couple of men walking slowly towards me at the other end of the grass section. They had their hands in the pocket of their trousers, lazily walking towards the edge of the cliff, looking out to sea. When they noticed I'd spotted them, they started to run, and not towards the cliffs but towards me. My heart jumped in my throat. I pulled my bag free and ran. I ran across the next field and instead of going through the gate, I scrabbled over the old rock fence. Some of the rocks fell loose against my abuse and fell to the ground. I could hear them behind me. I looked back. There were even more men after me, one of them had a dog. Pure fear ran through me. I bolted towards the archway entrance. I could feel my body getting its glow on. I ran faster up the wide concrete stairs. I felt a sharp pull on my foot as I touched the stone. I could hear Uar on the other side.

"Grab me Uar!"

I felt his hand as a stabbing pain exploded in my calf muscle.

I hung onto Uar as the spinning stopped and my mind refocused.

"You're bleeding."

"I'm bleeding? What?"

I looked down at my pounding calf. I'd felt that dog's jaw clamp down on my leg just as I jumped through the portal. "It was that bloody dog, Uar they knew I was coming here. They were there when I went to the castle, they chased me and their dog…"

"Shh" he hushed as he pulled me closer to him. He stroked my hair as my body melted into his. "You're safe now." He kept me tight against him for a few moments longer before he draped me in the familiar grey cloak and guided me towards the houses. "Let's get you indoors and we will see to that wound. If they know where you were going, they will be here soon."

I let him take me with him as my heart pounded. I knew they wanted to kill me, but this made it all so real. I had a dog bite to prove it and it really hurt. I could feel it pounding up my leg with every step I took. I hope Hayden was looking after my family. My Phone! I grabbed for my back pocket for my phone. I pulled it out. Dam! No signal. Of course there'd be no signal, I wasn't in Dunedin anymore, let alone New Zealand.

"What is that?" Uar asked me.

"It's my phone."

"What is a phone?"

How was I going to explain this? "Well, this allows me to talk to people that aren't here with me."

"What? You can talk to anybody on that phone from anywhere?"

"Well, as it turns out, not here. I have no bars, no signal. I can't contact anybody?"

"Bars?"

He looked confused, I changed the subject. There were a lot more things I'd need to explain first before I discussed the workings of a mobile phone. "Um, maybe we could discuss this another time. Let's just concentrate about getting me safe and not dead."

He pushed me faster down the back alley streets. We ducked and dove through some small alleyways, dodging the small amount of people as they walked gloomily by, not even giving us a second look. Life was bad here. We came to a dead end. Wooden barrels were stacked up against one of the walls. Uar pushed a couple away and knocked on the crude hidden wooden door twice and then three times slower than the first two. The door swung open.

"Uar! Did you get her?" A big burly man poked his head out. He took one look at me. "Aye, I think that is a yes, get yourselves inside, quick."

We were quickly shuffled into a small room that looked similar to the room I was in last time I was here. Uar held my hand the entire time. It felt like he didn't want to let it go. I appreciated his warmth and friendship, this was not my normal social situation and I wasn't sure what was going to happen.

"Uar!" shouted a group of people sitting on a long shared banquet table.

Uar pressed his fingers to his lips to shush them. He had a smile on his face. He was clearly happy to see them. I positioned myself slightly behind him. Who were these people? They all looked delighted to see us. They were dressed the same as Uar, all topless, except for the female that was beaming happily at me. She had on a gold breast plate of armour and her dark long hair was swept up in a high ponytail. A grey cape draped down her back. She looked every part of a warrior. She definitely belonged in this room. Everybody was huge and intimidating. I shrunk closer behind Uar's back.

"Brigid, this is the Gold Belts." He swept his arms out past them all to introduce them.

I waved sheepishly from behind his back. "Hi." My voice sounded stupid and weak. I was embarrassed and felt so small. They all looked like they belonged in the WWF wrestling arena.

They quickly jumped out of their seats and pushed and shoved each other to introduce themselves to me. I politely acknowledged them, forgetting all of their names instantly. I think there were about twelve people there, all huge warriors, with bulging muscles and they were all in skirts. They made those skirts look good though. There was a tall skinny one, that didn't seem overly happy to see me. When it was his turn to greet me, he just grunted. His name was Yute. That was the only name I remembered.

The female came up to me and looked me up and down with concern. "Uar, she is bleeding." She turned to me and took both my arms in her hands. "I'm going to put you on the stool beside the fire. Gurt, get the girl some mead to drink. Uar get over here."

A stocky dark haired man at the end of the table poured some liquid into a clay cup of me. I sat down on the stool and looked down at my leg. There was a large flap of skin folding down to my ankle. A pool of blood lined the floor. That dog had done a real number on me. I felt faint. I knew my leg hurt, but I hadn't realised it looked like this, it made it seem even worse. Uar was right, there were definitely people out there to kill me and in this case a dog.

The female gently turned my head to face her. "Uar is going to heal your leg, now it won't be completely healed, but enough so that it won't get infected. Are you ready?" I nodded. I could do this, I was a bit suspicious about Uar though - he could heal my leg? Seemed a bit unbelievable, but – wow! I took a sip from my drink. It was bitter sweet. It tasted good though. I nodded in acknowledgement. I was anxious, I didn't know what to expect. I knew there was a flap of skin hanging off my leg, had it torn my muscle? When did I have my last tetanus shot? OMG – was I going to get rabies? I was starting to panic. I took a huge gulp of my mead. It made me feel temporarily better. I clenched my teeth and waited for Uar to heal me, hoping it wasn't going to be painful.

Uar came over and placed both his hands over my calf. I winced at the pain as he pressed the flap of skin back in place. He closed his eyes and started chanting. I took another sip and closed my eyes. I felt the warmth instantly flow up my leg, it soothed me. I heard a combined intake of breath, but I ignored it and kept my eyes closed, savouring his touch. This feeling was amazing. I could feel light flowing out from me and my skin knitting itself together again. It was magical, this didn't hurt at all. I opened my eyes once Uar's touch left me and coldness washed over where his touch had been. I instantly missed it.

The whole room was staring at me. They had gotten off their seats and were crouched around me with their mouths wide open.

I suddenly felt self-conscious. "What?" I asked. They just sat there with their mouths dropped to the floor. They looked amazed. "What?" My heart started to race, what was wrong with me? Did it all go horribly wrong?

They all quickly scrambled to their seats again, ducking their heads and avoiding eye contact. They continued on, drinking their drinks as if nothing peculiar had just happened. I looked at Uar. He had a huge smile on his face.

"What?"

He kept smiling widely as he took my hands and pulled me up. "Come, let's sit."

He took me over to the table. Room was made for us both on the long wooden bench seats. Uar sat beside me and gently placed his hand on the small of my back to comfort me. I appreciated it. I could feel his strength and I needed it sitting next to these impressive people.

"So… Brigid?"

It was the female that spoke to me from across the table. I took another sip of my drink as she smiled at me. Everyone else was talking around us paying us no attention, except Yute. I could feel his stare without even looking at him. The female got up and made her way over to me, pushing the man beside me down the bench further so she could fit it. He grunted but quickly made room for her. She put an arm around my shoulder and I could feel the weight of it push me down. I straightened my back, not wanting her to think I was weak. I felt Uar rub my lower back before he pulled his hand away. I wanted to grab it and put it back where it was, I wanted to yell at him to keep it where it was, I needed its strength. I had no idea what this lady was going to do to me.

"Hagrid, pass me down my drink!" She yelled at a ginger haired man with a long bristly ginger beard. He pushed it down the table to her, she caught it and took an incredibly large gulp out of it.

"Now Brigid, let's talk."

I stared up at her golden brown almond shaped eyes that sloped upwards at the outer edges. I gulped. "Okay."

"Relax, I don't bite." She smiled at me, but I didn't relax. Somehow I felt like I was the lamb and she was the wolf about to eat me. "I just want to know a bit about you." She said sweetly as she looked down at my newly healed leg. My three quarter Lycra running pants were still intact with a few spots of blood on them. They were grey with a fluorescent pink line down the sides. I knew this was a colour that they wouldn't see often, if ever, in this place of the Otherworld. "How long have you known that you had our Mother's light inside you?"

I turned to Uar, wanting to gauge how he was reacting with her questioning me. He had his back to me, laughing with the man beside him. I turned back to her. "Well, I have only known for about a month now, so not long."

"Humph" she replied and looked intensely at me. "So, you mean to tell me that you've not realised for what, about twenty years that you are part Goddess?"

Twenty Years, I wasn't that old. "I'm only seventeen, so that would be for seventeen years, and no I didn't realise. I mean, my arm always discoloured into patterns when I'd been in the sun for too long, but eventually it would go away. I just thought I had some sort of skin allergy or something?"

"Interesting" she replied tapping her fingers on the wooden table. She smiled at me and gave me a hug. Obviously questioning was over. I felt her friendliness. "Do you know you just witnessed a miracle?"

"A miracle? Do you mean my leg being healed, because that *was* pretty amazing?" It was totally amazing. I still couldn't believe that there isn't even a scar on my leg.

"You should have a scar still on your leg. A red angry scar, it should not have completely healed, just enough for it to close over and so infection can't set in. Uar is good, but has been off his game since Mother was frozen. Part of her light left him then too, but you..." She hugged me again. "You've our Mother's light in you, that's proof. With Uar's power and yours – your leg healed completely! That's a wonderful outcome. Your whole body glowed, lit up the entire room - it was a miracle."

I heard a couple of cheers from the few men that had turned their attention to us. "Really, so this isn't normal? I mean my leg healing isn't normal? And I glowed?" That shocked me. My body had glowed! Next time, I'd have to keep my eyes open so I could check it out.

"No, well it used to be, but not anymore and it won't be again unless we restore order around here and yes you glowed! Shone up the whole god dam room."

Wow, I felt closer to Uar. Was it weird that I had feelings for Uar, when I had his mother's light inside me? Was I his mother? I knew technically I wasn't, but it still felt a bit weird. "Wow!" I said aloud as I looked down at my leg again. I did have power inside me like Uar said I did.

"Now, let's drink and eat while we can. Tomorrow we're going to train and figure out exactly how we're going to get our Mother back."

I smiled a fake smile as I inwardly convulsed with fear. I took a drink with everyone as they cheered, calling me the light bearer. Someone started singing and I was slowly forgotten about, left to my thoughts and the worry of having to save these people. That's not me, I can't save them, I've never done anything heroic in my life. How was I supposed to save them? Look at them, they're warriors. I do not look like them, I'm not them. I excused myself and went to sit down at the back of the small room. I opened my bag to get out a piece of chocolate. I needed sugar to help my nerves. I fumbled around in my overnight bag until I found what I was looking for and broke a piece off. I popped it in my mouth and savoured the sweet chocolatey taste. What was I doing here?

CHAPTER 13

Everyone was sleeping. I wasn't, I couldn't. The snoring around the room was keeping me up along with the expectations the Gold Belts had of me being their light bearer. People lay down where they could find a space and slept, weapons laid out beside them or under them, never too far away. Uar had given me a woollen blanket to wrap around myself, but the floor was too hard and the weight of what I was supposed to do hung heavily on me. I felt like a fraud. I thought about B and hoped he was alright. I felt bad about leaving him alone and giving him no explanation as to why or where I was going. I left Mum and Dad a note and hoped he had read it while they had slept. He'd be angry with me, and I hoped he'd still be there when I returned. The thought of him not being there when I got home broke my heart. I could hear the crackle of the fire from the centre of the room. I sat up and pushed my blanket back. Uar said I may have powers, time I checked it out and see whether I did or not. I glowed tonight and my leg healed completely, which apparently wouldn't have happened if not for the power within me. Uar once said I should try and talk to fire and it might talk back. Crazy, I know, but this last month has been crazy. There was a strange feeling inside me, an assertive feeling, a feeling of knowing - I think I already knew I could talk to fire. I sneakily looked around the room feeling odd about what I was about to do. Everyone was asleep and paying me no attention at all. Uar was asleep close beside me so I carefully stepped over him as I made my way to the fire. The hanging cauldron had been swung aside so it was not directly burning above the fire anymore. It still had last night's stew in it. The flames danced and spat in freedom as I approached. Once again I felt entranced. The memory of the bomb fire at Stephen's house came back to me - the feeling of belonging. Even then, I was entranced by them.

"Hello" I whispered quietly, feeling slightly foolish I was talking to the fire in the middle of the room. I quickly looked around again to see if anyone was watching and breathed a sigh of relief when I saw that they were all still sound asleep. I waited for a response from the fire, no answer. "Hello my name is Brigid." I repeated.

The flames reached out further to me. I could feel their warmth on my skin. "*Welcome home*" It whispered back to me in a slow hissed response.

I jumped back slightly. OMG, it worked. My heart raced, this was really happening. "Thanks." I replied quietly in total shock. I jumped again as I heard someone cough. I tiptoed quickly back to my spot on the floor all excited with myself. I could speak to fire. Eek! I wondered what it would say to me when I had time to talk to it properly, it was exciting. I closed my eyes and dreamt of dancing in a ballroom with flames and laughter. The little girl was there too, laughing with me. They were my friends and I felt completely safe with them.

I saw the ground coming closer to me before I felt it. Uar's hard body slammed on top of mine. I'd lost my balance and pulled Uar down with me. When my head cleared I smiled apologetically to him. He leaned closer to me. I could feel his breath touch my face. I thought he was going to kiss me. The heat rose up on my cheeks as I leaned closer.

"Uar, play nice!" Brea yelled. We both moved quickly away from each other. Scampering away like naughty little children. I found out the female's name after Uar said it in a passing comment. It was a nice name and it suited her completely.

Whatever that moment was, Brea had broken it. Uar sprung back to his feet and put his hand out to pull me up. "Sorry about that."

I huffed as I dusted the dirt off my clothes.

"It's just that, I don't know, but for some reason you are here and we are stronger, I can feel it through my body, I can feel the light through me, I nearly feel… back to my normal self – it's exhilarating."

I could see his excitement and smiled. It felt good to be making them feel better and apparently I was making them all feel real good. It was the light inside me reconnecting with them all again. They could feel it and they wanted it back. "I'm glad I'm doing some good" I replied as I heard the swords clanging in the background, because my fighting wasn't very good at least my presence was doing something.

Hagrid had the gift of illusion. He could make people see whatever he wanted them to see. He couldn't do it for long stretches of time anymore but because I was here, he was more powerful and reckoned that he could cloak us all while we trained so nobody could see us. We were somewhere just out of town in a meadow and no one could see us, we were completely invisible, how cool was that? The Gold Belts wanted to see what I was capable of before I was sent off on the mission, which apparently wasn't much. Nobody seemed to mind though except Yute, he kept staring at me and it was seriously starting to annoy me.

"What's his problem?" I angrily asked Uar. I stared at Yute's thin greasy blond hair. "Would it kill the man to wash his hair once in a while or to crack a smile?"

He turned to see who I was talking about. I heard a loud moan as Brea threw one of the men over her back to the ground. She smiled in triumph. She was good! "Don't worry about him Brigid." He looked disappointed. "He'll come around."

"But he keeps staring at me like he wants me dead, should I be worried?" And I wasn't sugar coating it, earlier he was sharpening his knifes as he looked directly at me. His thin greasy blond hair was pulled back loosely showing his gangly skinny neck. Seriously, did this guy ever blink?

"No need to be worried. He has some trust issues, that's all."

"Well that makes two of us."

"Right, again?" Uar said as he stood in his fighting stance. I rolled my eyes. I had told him I wasn't very good at this sort of thing, but he insisted he was going to show me how. I just rolled with the flow.

We sat down for some lunch. Hagrid needed a break so we walked deep into the dense forest. I sat down on the damp grass and welcomed the cool feeling against my bum. My muscles were going to be sore in the morning. I thought of myself as reasonably fit, but the workout I just had was intense, using muscles I was sure I'd never used before in my life.

"We need to come up with a plan" Brea announced as I was halfway through my oat biscuit.

"Yes we do" Gurt replied. He had crumbs all over his chest, mixed in with his dark salt and pepper chest hairs. He had long hair, held tightly back in a simple plait, a small amount of silver hair shone through his otherwise dark locks. "I can feel her already, with Brigid here, I can feel her."

Everyone murmured their agreeance except for Yute, he just huffed and threw a knife into the trunk of a tree across from him. I jumped at the sound it made as it pierced through the innocent tree. He was dangerous and I needed to stay clear of him. Brea rolled her eyes at him. "We need to get Brigid to the Oak trees and we need to come up with a plan of how we are going to do that. They already know she's here, I felt their evil intent in my sleep last night. They will be ready waiting for us." Brea was a deity goddess, kind of like Uar, except her speciality was warfare, she was a warrior goddess. How cool was that? If there was any power I could have, it would secretly be a warrior. I shrunk closer to the tree trunk I was leaning against. Once again, we were talking about me saving them, saving their mother and it freaked me out! I was nothing except a vessel that was holding their Mother's light inside me, somewhere, somehow her light was hiding in me and for once, I wished it would go away and find someone else.

"I can always cloak us" Hagrid said, "but that will be harder when the fighting starts trying to focus on everyone as we get split up."

"Yes, maybe, but they will be expecting that, they know that you will be with us. We will certainly try it though. It's a good start." Uar said as he stood up and stretched out his back. "There's only one way to get to the Oak Trees and the Fomorians know it and it will be blocked."

Gurt spat on the ground next to him when Uar mentioned the word Fomorians. No one paid him any notice.

"We need to… " Uar stopped in mid-sentence and crouched low to the ground. "Shh" he grabbed for his sword. "Hagrid?" he whispered urgently.

Everyone shut up instantly as Hagrid cloaked us against the voices that were walking our way. I couldn't make out what they were saying, but by the expressions of the Gold Belts, they were not good news. This was the enemy, they must have been the Fomorians. I could feel the tension in the air. The voices got louder as they came closer. I could hear the breaking of twigs as one of them entered my view. I took a sharp intact of breath. His grotesque head spun around at the noise. Everyone stared at me giving me death looks. I could have just blown our cover. He was disgusting, he moved closer to me sniffing. He certainly couldn't see me, but it knew something wasn't right. His face was covered in large protruding boils and his left shoulder hung lower than his right which had multiple lumps poking out of it making his red cape lopsided. I held my breath and closed my eyes as he moved even closer, I could smell his rancid breath. He held his hand out towards me, feeling the air for something he couldn't see. I leaned slowly to my left side as he kept moving towards the tree I was leaning against. More of them came into view, each as ugly and grotesque as the next.

"Roc!" one of them yelled. "Get a move on."

He took a big sniff as he closed his eyes. After a few moments he shook his head and limped away. Nobody moved until they were well away from us.

"Well done Hagrid" Brea whispered as she sunk her head down on her knees breathing a sigh of relief. "They could have found her."

"Yes well done" Uar followed. "They must be closing in their ranks and calling in for reinforcements. They're getting ready for us."

I had tears running down my face. I was freaking out. That thing nearly had me. I looked around and everyone was keeping their own kind of calm and I was going to do the same. I will inwardly freak out! Uar took my hand and pulled me up. "I think we need to get you some different clothes, clothes that don't... glow."

I looked down at the fluorescent pink strip down my leg and silently agreed he was right.

"Let's move. We need to get to our Mother before she's completely surrounded." Someone said from the group.

"Agreed" Uar said. "Brigid, are you okay?"

"No!" I said. "What were those things? Were they the Fomorians, the ones that I'm supposed to conquer?" I could feel my body shaking, I was losing it. So much for me only *inwardly* freaking out.

He looked at me glumly and nodded his head.

"Look I get it, I need to do this and I will, but you need to know something. Where I come from, there are no Fomorians, I don't need to save the world so I've never trained for it. My biggest concern is getting my homework in on time or making sure Winkles my cat has food in her bowl, I'm not used to this, this isn't how I was brought up so if you think that I'm suddenly going to be an awesome warrior, you're wrong - that isn't me." I took deep breaths, don't faint Brig don't faint. I was willing myself to stay upright. I had just admitted to these amazing *god* people that I wasn't good enough to do the job I was born to do and they just stared at me.

They all slowly stood up and brushed the dirt off themselves, fobbing me off. No one believed me or cared that I was freaking out. They all got to work packing away the leftover food and ignored me completely. How was I going to get through to them, I was not the one to save them. Yes I had the light of their Mother inside me, but I was no warrior. All of a sudden I felt alone. I wished Hayden was here with me. He'd have my back. He would say something to make me laugh and everything would be okay. What was I doing here?

"Let's pick this back up at the safe house." Brea said. "We need to make a plan and we need to do it now, you all know what's going on, they're closing ranks. They know she's here. We need to move and we need to move now!"

Everyone agreed and moved quickly. I felt a sharp nudge against my shoulder as Yute walked past me. "I knew you wouldn't handle this. You're going to bring us all down with you." He spat on the ground beside me "you're just the same." He walked away after giving me the death stare. I wanted to burst into tears, but I held them back and didn't respond to him. He was right. I was - I couldn't do this, who was I kidding? I was Brigid from Dunedin. I was nothing special. I hung my head and followed behind them all. Even Uar didn't walk with me, and I didn't mind. I needed space to wallow in my own self-pity. I had to get back up, I had to do this. It was my life too and for some reason this was my destiny. I was going to have to embrace it and become a warrior because I'd be damned if I was going to die by the hand of some disgusting grotesque Fomorian! I pulled my shoulders back and walked faster. I caught up with the group and nudged Uar. He turned and smiled at me. He must've felt my decision. He had faith in me so I should have faith in myself. I was going to save them and their Mother, I could do this, I was the light bearer.

CHAPTER 14

Once again I found myself staring into the fire pit back at the safe house. We'd come up with a plan and we were going to leave before first light tomorrow. Everyone was to get a few hours' sleep before we left. Everyone except for me - I couldn't sleep. I felt like I was walking into my death bed. Could I survive this? The graceful movements of the fire comforted me. I grabbed my blanket and quietly dragged it to the fire. I wrapped it around myself as the flames leaned gently towards me.

"What am I going to do?" I asked the flames in a whisper. "I don't think I can do this. I can't fight, I can't really do anything?"

The flames leaned over further and brushed my wrist. I pulled away waiting for the burn, but nothing happened. It didn't hurt. I held my hand out and the flame was drawn to it. A small part broke off and stayed in the palm of my hand. I watched in awe as it danced around comforting me. "*You can do something*" it quietly hissed.

"What?"

"*What are you doing now?*"

"Holding fire in my hand."

"*Yes and how are you doing that?*"

I didn't really know. "Has it got something to do with the light inside me?" It looked like it nodded. It dawned on me. Brigid was the bearer of light, she can control fire. "Can I control fire?" I asked the little flame dancing around on my hand.

"*Yesss*" it hissed gently.

"But how?"

"*Use your mind.*"

Use my mind? Okay. I focused on my little flame child. Nothing happened. I huffed. I shook my head, no, I wasn't going to give up. I have to do this, I have no choice so I may as well contribute and try. I closed my eyes and focused again. I slowly opened my eyes. I let out a loud Eek! The flame was floating above my hand. "I did it" I lowered my voice not wanting to wake anybody. "I did it" I whispered again to my baby flame. It did a little dance for me before it jumped back into the fire.

"Well done!" Uar quietly clapped behind me.

I spun around shocked he'd been watching me. "What? You saw that?"

"Yes, I saw it. How did it feel?"

"It felt amazing! I can't explain it, I can just think about what I want it to do and it just did it and it felt right… it was weird, but in a good way."

He sat down beside me and rested his leg against mine as we both looked into the fire. Inwardly I was doing high fives with myself.

I wanted to keep going and see how far I could go with this. "I appreciate what you are doing Brigid. You don't have to help us, but you are and for that I thank you, we all thank you."

I sat there looking at my new friend, the fire. "I kind of have to."

"You don't, not if you didn't want to, we would never force you… well Brea might." He smiled with the mention of her name.

"I didn't mean it like that. What I meant was, I have this precious gift inside me, your Mother's light and in a way, my Mother's too. It's in me for a reason. I just needed to come to terms with what was expected of me. I just didn't know how I was going to do it and what it all meant. I was afraid, actually I'm still afraid."

He put his arm around me and gave me a squeeze. "It's okay to be afraid."

"I know that now thanks."

"If you weren't afraid, I would be worried."

"Are you afraid?"

"Yes I am, very afraid. I'm afraid of the journey and I'm afraid of the outcome. What if it doesn't work? What if I let you down?"

"What?! You can't let me down, look at you – you are like, a god warrior person. I'm afraid I'm going to let you down, let everybody down. I don't contribute anything. You all have amazing gifts, and most importantly you all know how to fight, I have no idea about any of that sort of thing."

"You do contribute Brigid, you do. You have the light and that is the most important thing. That is the whole reason we are all here. You held the fire before, some of Mother's abilities have transferred to you also. You have abilities that you may not be aware of yet."

I nodded in agreeance. I did hold the fire, what else was I able to do? I was looking forward to finding out. But for now I needed sleep. "Hey" I turned to Uar. "Have you ever heard of Chocolate?"

"Chocolate? No, I don't think so. What is it?" He looked confused.

"Just you wait and see." I grabbed my bag and brought if over to the fire. I opened the zip and looked around for my Mum's chocolate I grabbed as I ran out the door the other day. If he hadn't tried chocolate before, this was going to blow his mind. His reaction was going to be awesome! I moved my hand around the inside of my bag. I couldn't feel it. I opened the zip further and peeked in. Empty packets were everywhere. "What?" I urgently moved all of the empty packets to the side, I have hardly been in my bag since I'd been there. Where was my chocolate? I kept searching, I felt something warm and soft under my hand. I peeled back the empty wrappers. "B!"

He snorted as he rolled over and scratched his stomach. His eyes slowly opened. He jumped up when he saw me staring down at him. He'd been caught. "What are you doing here B?" I whispered between clenched teeth.

"Is everything okay?" Uar asked as he looked over my shoulder. "Zeg!"

B looked up at Uar with a huge smile and scampered up my arm to get to Uar. They must know each other? Zeg?

"Zeg, what are you doing here? I haven't seen you for… well, for a very long time."

B motioned to his throat. "That's right, you can't talk anymore." B nodded his head sadly, but then his smile came back. "It's so good to see you, Mother will be happy you are here."

"Mother? Do you know B?" This had me floored. First of all B was here, second B's name was actually Zeg, and he knows Uar.

"Yes, Zeg was Mother's brownie. Zeg lived with her, helped her. They were good friends."

"Wow! What a small world."

They both looked at me strangely. "Sorry, it's a saying from where I come from. Wow!" I turned to B. "So your name is Zeg."

He was now sitting on Uar's shoulder. He nodded his head at me as his large pointy ears bounced with the movement.

"Nice to meet you Zeg." I held out my hand and laughed as he held my little finger for a hand shake.

"Zeg helped my Mother try and get away from the Fomorians before they could get to her. They froze Zeg's voice at the same time Mother was frozen. Zeg jumped in the way." Zeg bowed his head and shook it. He was clearly upset about it. Uar gave him a little nudge, "You did the best you could do. You were there and you helped. The forces of the Fomorians were too strong, you did your best Zeg and I'm sorry you lost your voice and I'm sorry for not being there."

Zeg looked up at Uar with his big black eyes glistening. He quickly wiped away his tears, embarrassed that he was crying. So that's why he couldn't talk. What a personality Zeg was, loyal and furious. He'd tried to save Brigid and lost his voice for his efforts. I wondered if his voice would come back when Brigid came back. Was that something I could do? If we were successful tomorrow, getting Zeg's voice back was going to be first on my list of things to do.

We talked for a while longer before we tried to get some sleep. Before I knew it, Uar was getting everyone up. I closed my eyes again, wishing it was the weekend and wishing I was at home in my comfy double bed and I could go back to sleep and forget about all of this. But the reality was, I couldn't. It was "D" day today, today was the day!

There was a knock at the door. Everybody froze. There was another double knock a few seconds later. Uar let out a breath of relief. "It will be Tunnan."

A man walked in, a handsome man with long dark wavy hair, held half up in a leather tie. He swung his cape off as everybody welcomed and greeted him. He had a bow and arrow strapped against his back and a smaller one on his side. He had daggers strapped up his leather pants. Yes, his chest was bare, like everybody else's here in the Otherworld and he had on a large ring with a huge blue stone in the centre of it. Tunnan certainly knew how to make an entrance.

Once everyone had greeted him, he made his way over to me. I was sitting on the ground and he towered over me with his hands on his hips. "And you must be Brigid?"

"Yes she is" Uar replied for me as he made his way over to us.

I was feeling small and stood up. He still towered over me, they both did. "Nice to meet you Brigid." He held out his hand and I shook it.

"Nice to meet you too."

"Thanks for coming Tunnan, we all appreciate it." Uar slapped him on the back.

"Of course. If she…" pointing to me "can change this place I'm all for a bit of sunshine in my life." He gave me a glare. He didn't seem convinced I was the one for the job. I held out my hand as part of the fire jumped onto it. I twisted it around my wrist as he stared at it. I could feel Tunnan's surprise. "Well maybe there is hope after all." He smiled and nodded his head in acknowledgement to me.

I smiled smugly as he walked away.

"When did you learn that?" Brea asked as she made her way to my side strapping on her belt.

"Last night." I gave her the biggest smile. "Pretty cool aye!"

"Yes, whatever *cool* means." She laughed. "I'm glad, you seem to be happy today, more assertive. It's reassuring."

I did feel better today. I can manipulate fire, B... I mean Zeg was here. Even though I should be mad at him for stowing away, but I was actually secretly happy. He was still sleeping in my bag. I felt confident. "I am" I simply said to her.

"What's Tunnan's deal anyway?" I looked in his direction as he talked to Uar.

"Tunnan is a complicated one. His archery skills are legendary though and he's a formidable warrior with exact precision, he never misses. There was a sense of relief when he walked in before, you would have felt it. Everybody knows we have a better chance with Tunnan with us and I'm glad for it. I will talk to you later about it, but for now, let's get ready to go. It's still dark outside, but it's getting lighter. We need to have the element of surprise because they will be waiting for us and I need to let Tunnan know what we have planned, we cannot fail today."

CHAPTER 15

I strapped on my chest armour that Brea had given me to wear. It felt cold and hard against my skin. I'd opted for leather leggings rather than the familiar skirt they all wore. I had a picture of a cute little pug dog wearing a pink tiara on the front of my knickers. Slightly embarrassing if I fell over or died with my skirt above my head. Tight leather leggings = embarrassing knickers never being seen. My underwear choice had not entered my mind when I packed for this adventure. Zeg had wanted to come with me. If I'd said no, he would have stowed away anyway. So I didn't argue and let him come along. I wrapped a long piece of cloth over my shoulder and around my waist then tucked him into it. He was on the outside of my armour, so I had to make sure I protected him. He was as snug as a bug in a rug at the moment and I could feel his snores ringing gently against my armoured chest. As well as my small dagger, I'd also asked for a bow and arrow. I knew I could shoot one and my chances of survival would go up. Tunnan reluctantly sacrificed one of his small ones to me and I strapped it comfortably on my back. It felt familiar and I felt slightly more warrior like with it on.

"Do you know how to use one of those?" Tunnan asked from behind me.

I jumped and put my hand on my heart as I spun around. "My god, Tunnan - you scared me."

He stared at me. "There are a lot more scarier things than me out there. Let's hope for all of our sakes you don't scare so easily on the field or we're all dead."

Anger boiled up inside me. I had just gotten my mind to a place that was prepared to fight today and in one foul swoop, Tunnan had fractured it. "For your information, I can use a bow and arrow and the only reason I jumped was because of your stench – it is repulsive."

I walked away with my head held high and left him with his mouth hanging open. Of course he didn't stink, but it was the first thing that came into my head to momentarily hurt him for making me doubt myself again. I smirked and kept walking. I heard some of the men snigger and it made my smile grow. Water burst out of Uar's mouth in surprise as he laughed out loud. He put his cup of water down and wiped his chin. He nodded his head to me and I nodded back. He had acknowledged how awesome I just was. I was ready to fight, I was ready to win.

Sweat dripped down my forehead and my heart pounded. This was it… this was the day I could possibly die. Hay tickled my cheeks as I lay tummy down on the ground glaring out at the Fomorians. They had made camp in the field of hay, directly in front of the Oak Trees. Small red square tents were pitched everywhere. No pattern, just everywhere. Grotesque Fomorian's sat by their small campfire's cooking meat and drinking. Some wandered around chatting to each other. They didn't look prepared or scared. It was like we didn't matter to them and they were just getting on with their daily lives. That was a bit off putting – because I was certainly scared of them and as for the preparation, I sincerely hoped we were.

"Is this normal?" I whispered to Uar. "I mean they don't look scared at all. I on the other hand feel like I'm going to wet my pants with fear." I instantly regretted telling him that. I needed to think more before I spoke. How embarrassing!

He pushed my head down gently and put his finger up to his lips. "We have the upper hand, don't worry." He looked at Brea and she nodded. She pointed to Tunnan and he split off from the group.

"Where's he going?" I asked Uar. This wasn't part of the plan.

"He's going to scout the area." He looked worried. I matched his expression. "Don't worry Tunnan's our best hunter, he won't be seen."

I leaned up from the ground slightly as I felt a tap on my armour. I must've been squashing Zeg. I gave him a gentle rub as an apology. "What now... do we just wait?"

Uar nodded.

Great, I was in no hurry to die. This would do for now. I relaxed a bit and felt for my bow and arrow. Yip, it was still there. I wished I had time to practice with it. All bows are different, but until Tunnan walked through the door, I didn't know they had any, which was stupid now that I think about it, how would they hunt and Hayden, Hayden was a great shot at archery, and of course he was because he was from the Otherworld. I missed Hayden, I wish he was with me. I have some major apologising to do when I get back. He will not be happy I just ran out on him like this.

I felt a tap on my back. It was Uar. He was pointing to Tunnan, he was back. That was fast. He whispered something to Gurt then turned to the rest of the warriors behind us and pointed up. Around fifty other people joined us this morning. All ready and eager for this curse to be over. Gurt whispered down the line. When it got to me

Brea whispered *"They are waiting in the trees, Hagrid will cloak us from above but be prepared."* I looked into the trees surrounding the hay field, I couldn't see anyone. I passed the message on to Uar. He held up his fingers for the front line to see and dropped them slowly one at a time. When his last finger dropped he started crawling along the hay, moving towards the Fomorians. I slowly followed as did the rest of the group. I made sure I lagged slightly behind Uar, being in front was not a priority of mine, I wanted

to savour the small amount of time I had left. I shook my head. I needed a mental check on myself. I needed positivity. I was their saviour, somehow this was supposed to work out... wasn't it?

We slowly moved on. I kept my eye on Uar. He looked like a natural at this. He was flat against the ground, his muscles holding him up. He looked like he was barely moving. Then there was me, barrelling ungracefully through the hay, how they didn't hear me I had no idea. Maybe Hagrid could disguise sound as well? I doubted that though. I could see Uar's chiselled thighs and his muscles contracting as he pushed his body to the limits and closer to the camp. What a sight he was. He quickly spun around to me. I looked in the other direction hiding my red face. He must've sensed me checking him out. He smiled and put his finger to his mouth. Of course, it was my ungraceful noise that gave me away. I gave him an apologetic facial expression in return. Hey, it's not my fault I wasn't a natural at this sort of thing. I started to smell the smoke from the camp fires. We must be close. I didn't dare poke my head above the long hay to check it out. My trust was in Uar and when he moved, I moved.

It seemed to take forever to get there and with each crawl we took, my heart pounded harder. We finally reached the first tent. The hay had been trampled here by the Fomorians footsteps. There was nowhere for us to hide anymore. Uar crawled out of the long hay first and slowly stood up. We all stayed where we were. I couldn't see Uar's face I was too scared to look up. I was waiting for the war cry of the

Fomorians, but there was nothing. Uar was relying on Hagrid cloaking us so they couldn't see us. We had to do this in an orderly quiet fashion. Hagrid was only one person; if we all got split up he couldn't keep track of us all. Everyone slowly stood up. I followed very slowly. My breath caught in my chest. Three metres away were two Fomorians. Uar put his finger to his lips again, reminding me to be quiet. He wiggled his finger for me to follow him. Brea did the same to the rest of the group. One of the Fomorians was picking his toe nails and had his foot up on a piece of wood beside the camp fire. Yuck, I wanted to vomit. His calf was showing and the boils of oozing pus were disgusting. The other one had his red cape draped over his chest with its eyes closed. He was the dangerous one, was he pretending or was he really asleep? Eek, I slowly tiptoed past them. No movement. Hagrid's illusion was working. I just had to be as quiet as a mouse and as slow as a turtle. I followed behind Uar. We dodged tents left and right, there was no main walkway. I bet they did this because they knew Hagrid would be with us. It's harder to focus if we are constantly moving in and out and away from each other. We kept moving slowly and in an orderly fashion. At one point I had to stop quickly as a short Fomorian rushed out of his tent and emptied his bladder on the ground outside. I cringed as he made his way back into the tent. He was so close to me, I could smell his urine. I noticed he had his sword still attached to him. Uar noticed too and widened his eyes at me. We had to be careful, they were ready for us. I heard some dogs barking in the distance. Great, they had dogs. If the Fomorians looked like this, imagine what their dogs looked like. I didn't want to find out.

What seemed like an eternity, we finally got to a point where I could see the dark path between the Oak trees, where the bones of judgement would be. What if I couldn't get through again? It was a slow process but it was working. The Fomorians did not know we were there. Uar turned to me and took my hand. He pulled me closer to him as we approached the bones of judgement. I could hear their calls and I could feel the pull to get to the Oak trees. My head started to spin. I was where I needed to be. I felt my arm starting to glow. I looked desperately at my arm. I hadn't thought about that. My armour didn't cover my arms. The glow reached my hand and the pattern of flames shone out.

"Brigid!" someone yelled.

I spun around as Uar pushed me over the threshold. I bounced off it and landed on my bum.

"Stop! Brigid!"

Who was calling my name? It was familiar, I knew that voice. Then all chaos broke loose. Uar picked me up and threw me over his shoulders. I gagged as the breath left my chest with the force of falling on the ground. Uar had been hit by an arrow. It was sticking out of his shoulder. Oh god, no.

"No! Uar!" I screamed. I lay on top of him to shield him. Uar's warriors were in full force creating a wall around us. "Uar!"

He took my hand "Go Brigid, go now!"

"No! I won't leave you!"

"Go!" he screamed as he pushed me away. "I'll be fine."

I stood up. There was a thin wall of Uar's warriors and what looked like a sea of Fomorians. They were dropping like flies. I could see Tunnan up in the trees, firing his arrows and knocking the enemy down. His archery style reminded me of Hayden's, so similar.

Brea ran up to me. "Go Brigid, go! You must get to our Mother. We will hold them off."

A huge dog jumped over the sea of Fomorians and Brea struck it down with her dagger straight into its skull as another grabbed onto her leg and pulled her down. I had to do something. I was the saviour, I had the light. I spun around in the chaos and saw Yute on the ground with a huge Fomorian on him. Yute looked spent as the Fomorians blade was slowly piercing his skin on his chest. Yute was holding it up but the Fomorian was too strong and the laws of gravity were winning. Without thinking, I grabbed an arrow and shot. I saw the look of astonishment on Yute's face as the Fomorian collapsed on top of him with an arrow poking out of his eye. He looked at me, but I didn't have time to respond, I had to do something and quickly. I looked at the fires around the camp. An idea formed in my head. I closed my eyes and willed them all to me. I kept my eyes closed and imagined a wall of fire between us and the Fomorians. I could feel the stretching of my light take over the meadow and the pulling as I pulled the fire to where I wanted it to go. I heard screaming as I opened my eyes. It worked! It worked! I did a wee jump of excitement! It had actually worked! A huge wall of fire now separated us. I could feel its powerful heat and wanted to pull it into myself for comfort. I could hear the screams of the enemy as they were burnt by their own fires that were willed to me, doing what I wanted them to do. There was something unfamiliar within the fire, an unfamiliar power. I turned around and could see Uar holding his hand out while he held his bleeding shoulder with the other. He was helping me. He was helping me hold the wall of fire. The wall wobbled as I lost concentration and a handful of Fomorians got through. Brea and her crew sorted them out quickly, but I had to stay focused. Our success was riding on getting us all safely through the bones of judgement.

"Go!" I called out to Brea. "Go!" I nodded towards the dark path.

"No! You need to go first! You're too important." She called out as she wiped her blade clean against her thigh.

I looked at the wall. If I went first, everyone would die. I had to keep this up and get everyone through. I'd bolt at the end and hope that the bones will let me through otherwise I was a goner. "I can't, I have to hold this wall up. If I lose concentration it will come down."

She grimaced. She knew I was right.

"I will stay!"

I looked at Uar.

"I'll stay with her." His healing powers must've kicked in as he wasn't holding his shoulder anymore. Both of his hands were out like mine helping to control the wall of fire. "Go! Go now!" I could feel his power as he yelled at Brea.

She nodded and yelled at everyone to go through. I could feel the relief as the last ones went through, they were safe. "Right Brig, you can let go. Let's go!" Brea ran through the path as I looked at Uar.

I dropped the wall and turned to run.

"Brig!" That voice was yelling at me again. It was instinct to turn as my name was being called. I turned and froze. Walking towards me from beyond the wall of ash was Hayden.

"Hayden!" My heart skipped a beat. "Hayden, run! Get out of here." I started to run towards him. What was he doing here? I grabbed my bow and arrow, ready to protect him.

"Brigid, run!" I could hear Uar as he tried to pull me back.

"No, I have to save him! He doesn't know what's going on!" I pulled away from Uar.

I stopped. Something didn't feel right. Hayden was walking towards me. I watched the Fomorians, the enemy, step aside to let him pass. "What?" It was like slow motion, they were letting him pass, why would they do that?

Uar grabbed me around my waist and lifted me towards the bones and shouted, "That's not Hayden, that's Cichol – we have to go! Now!"

"Let her go!" Hayden boomed. I felt the blast of power as Uar flew through the air, as he dropped me I felt familiar arms wrap around me. "Sorry Brig" I heard whispered in my ear, then complete darkness flooded me as pain exploded in my brain.

CHAPTER 16

My head was pounding and I was cold. I must be coming down with something. How inconvenient it was to get a cold during summer. Mum would know what to do. She'd give me some of her vitamins and tuck me up in bed. I stretched and tested my muscles. They hurt, but I had to get up and tell Mum I wasn't feeling well so she could sort me out. She'll know what to do. A few of those vitamins and back to bed for me and I'd be good as gold in a few days, maybe even tomorrow I'd be feeling better. I sat up and opened my eyes. It was dark, but I could see shadows in the distance. A creepy feeling ran down my back, I was not in my room! A flood of terror rushed through me. I was captured! Hayden! Oh my god Hayden captured me! He hit me around the head and captured me. Pure hatred took over my body. How could he?! He was my best friend! He knew my family. He played PlayStation with my brother! What was his deal? I couldn't believe my best friend would do this to me. Everything I knew about him was a lie, he lied to me about everything. Hayden must've told the Fomorians where I was when I text him about protecting my family, what a lying pig! I was so mad! I lay back down. It was hard and cold. I felt the floor with my hand. It was cold damp stone. I was locked in a cold damp stone prison… thanks a lot Hayden. "You wait until I see you again" I whispered to myself. My mind filled itself with revenge plots. I was going to get him back for this. I wished my Mum really was here with her vitamins. Zeg! Oh my god, Zeg was wrapped against me during the battle. I felt frantically around my chest, there was nothing there. He wasn't here. He had helped, but where was he now? My armour had gone and instead I was wearing some rough tunic over my leather leggings. I hoped he was okay and managed to get away. Oh Zeg, I'd never forgive myself if something happened to him. I felt lonely and stupid. Stupid for believing in Hayden, stupid for thinking he was my best friend and that he'd always have my back no matter what. Now, I'm in a stinking cold prison with no idea where I am. Tears started to fall. Did anyone even know where I was? Did Uar know where I was? Would he save me or would he think I was a lost cause? I needed to feel his strength, his light, I needed him. He has to come and get me. He'd come and get me, I was sure of it. But what if he couldn't, what if he can't find me. My family would be devastated that I never made it home. They will search for me but they will never find me. I wasn't even in the same dimension as them. I was stuck in the Otherworld, in a cold stoned prison, with no light, no fresh air – nothing.

I reopened my eyes when I felt a shadow fall over me. I quickly leapt up and scratched. I scratched and kicked with all I could. I heard laughter… they were laughing at me!

"Arghhhhhhh!" I screamed and spat at them and kicked again. I felt something soft against my kick as I was picked up and thrown against the cold hard wall. I fell in a heap on the ground.

"Keep that up missy and I won't feed ya."

"I don't care" I whispered mostly to myself. It was true, I didn't care. My whole world had just come crushing down on me. I heard a metal hinge lock as the heavy footsteps left me alone. I rubbed my shoulder and collapsed into myself.

"I told ya, she hasn't eaten. She's a witch! She kicked me in ma privates."

I heard a snigger. "Maybe she's a witch, maybe she might turn ya into a soft lazy cow like ya are."

A fist hit flesh as a fight broke out in my prison cell. I sat up and pushed myself to the corner of my cell. It was lighter now and I could see the huge Fomorians pounding fists into each other. Both had large deformities on their bodies with lumps and boils everywhere. They both had red capes draped over their shoulders. The larger one had the short fatter one in a choke hold and its face was turning purple, he was about to pass out. Good I thought to myself, and I hoped he cracked his head open on the way down.

"Enough!" Someone bellowed from the doorway. They both scampered to the far wall and bowed. It was Hayden. "Leave us!" The two guards quickly left.

I turned my back to him and wrapped my arms around my knees. I felt his hand gently touch my shoulder. "How could you?" I asked him quietly. "How could you?"

"Brig... I"

"How could you!" I screamed. I suddenly attacked him. I kicked and punched. I wanted to rip his eyes out. I did everything I possibly could to hurt him in my blind anger. "How could you! You were my best friend! You were my maths partner!" I grabbed his hair, yanked his head down and I punched him in the nose. He didn't even flinch. He wrapped his arms around me holding me down. I tried to kick, to scratch his eyes out but he had me bound tightly with this arms. He sat us awkwardly down on the ground and wrapped his legs around me too. I managed to get my foot out as I kicked it into his shin. He wrapped it back around and I was trapped, trapped between Hayden's arms and legs, and there was no getting out. They were like metal vices.

Tears were streaming down my face, anger was controlling me at the moment and all my anger wanted to do was to hurt Hayden. He held me tighter and started rocking me. My arms and legs were trapped under his and he had my head trapped under his own head. He shushed me gently as he rocked and started to whisper sweet calming words into my ear. Against my will I started to feel myself calm down. I started to rock with him and I cried. I cried until there were no more tears. He stayed with me, not saying a word and not letting me go.

Hayden broke the silence between us. "It wasn't supposed to be like this Brig."

"Yeah Hayden, well how was it supposed to be, you tell me."

"You were supposed to stay in Dunedin. You were supposed to stay safe. I gave you that bracelet to stop you from leaving. Nothing was supposed to get to you. All you had to do was keep my bracelet on, but instead you had to be a hero didn't you."

I huffed. I didn't care what he said. I didn't take that bracelet off by choice, hell I couldn't even remember taking it off, it was in the sink in a bowl of salty water when I woke up the morning after he gave it to me. "You lied to me Hayden, or should I call you Cichol."

He stopped rocking when I said his real name and paused. "You know."

"I do now!" I could feel the anger boil back up in me. "You had me believe that Uar was Cichol, that he was the one that was going to betray me, but no – it was you! You were Cichol all along. You're the betrayer. You want me dead!"

"Brig listen to me…"

"Cichol!"

He let go of me as he jumped to his feet. He wiped the dirt off his leather tunic and looked undisturbed. "She went berserk, she needed calming."

The man talking to Cichol was definitely the man in charge. Authority oozed out of him. I could practically smell it. He had a metal Viking hat on top of his long wavy blond hair that hung over his shoulders. There were two horns poking out from the top of his hat. His brown leather vest was made with the texture and design of scales. He was extremely handsome, in an old man kind of way. I felt entranced by him, he was magnificent. There was a feeling of intelligence about him and coldness, total utter coldness. Then I remembered where I was and he was quite possibly the reason I was in this hell hole. I stood up and held my head up high. This magnificent man was not going to get to me. I looked at Hayden, I mean Cichol. He hung his head in a submissive stance. This big Viking man was clearly his boss. Hayden looked different. He looked bigger. He was wearing similar clothing to the Viking and it was odd not seeing him in his jeans and faded t-shirt. His muscles were larger, he looked bigger, taller even. He turned and looked at me. No feelings on his face. I was just a piece of dirt to him. I snarled at him.

"So, this is her" the leader pointed to me. "She is the one to bring me down."

Cichol nodded but didn't say anything.

The leader came over to me, grabbed my chin and looked in to my eyes. His eyes were a deep dark blue and they bore into mine right down to my soul. I did my best not to look away. "She doesn't look like much." He shoved my chin away roughly and broke eye contact. "But I suppose they never do."

He clicked his fingers and a deformed Fomorian came in with a chair. He placed it down behind the leader as he sat down. The chair groaned under his weight. "Right, let's get down to business." I gulped. This did not sound good. I've watched movies and I knew this wasn't going to end well for me. "Brigid?" he looked at Cichol for confirmation of my name and Cichol nodded. "You have the same name as my ex-wife, how cliché."

Then it dawned on me. My captor was Bres, Uar's father. I didn't say anything to him but held my head up high. I didn't dare look at Cichol. Not that he would care anyway.

Bres clicked his fingers twice. A Fomorian appeared with a small wooden table and sat it down in front of him. A second Fomorian appeared with another chair and stopped in front of Bres. Bres nodded towards me and the Fomorian made his way over to me with the chair. He placed the chair down behind me. I spun around and kicked the chair into the Fomorian's shins. He let out a howl as my head slammed into the small wooden table. Bres lowered his head to my ear as his enormous hand squeezed my head against the wood. "Do that again and I'll tie you up… do you want that?"

I snarled at him and twisted to get out of his hold.

"I said DO YOU WANT THAT!"

I flinched. My ears were ringing as his screaming words buried their way into my head and banged against the sides. Bres was going to kill me, of that I was sure. I relaxed under his grip and he let my head go.

"Now I suggest you take the chair I have so graciously given you or I will tie you up and you can sit on the hard cold floor."

I slowly stood up and stared at him trying to hold back my tears.

"DO YOU UNDERSTAND?"

I flinched as his powerful voice boomed through my prison room. I nodded my head and sat down. I could feel my body shaking.

He tapped his fingers on the table. "I have a problem Brigid" he said gently. "I'm hungry!" He blurted out. He clicked his fingers and trays of food came out. "What about you? Brigid are you hungry?" He laughed "Of course you are, look at you. You are in my prison and I feed you when I want to!" He leaned forward and stared at me. I held his stare. I didn't know what to say. Was this a trick? He laughed again. "Go. Eat. Eat with me Brigid."

I starred at Cichol. He starred back with a blank expression with his hands behind his back as if he was standing guard. He didn't care.

Bres saw where I was looking. "Cichol! Come join us. Eat, you deserve it. Look at what you've brought me... my treasure." He laughed as he clicked his fingers again. A chair came and Cichol sat at the table between Bres and I.

Bres and Cichol dug in. There was so much food. Roast meat, vegetables, breads and sweets. I didn't know what to do. I still thought this was a trick. If I reached out for some food, would Bres chop my hand off? He did say for me to eat and I was starving. I didn't know what to do.

"What's the matter? You don't like my food I have kindly provided you?" Bres asked.

"No, I... I just don't know if you're tricking me or not."

He boomed with laughter again. "Cichol, get this useless girl some food... for some reason she doesn't trust me."

I turned to Cichol with death eyes. He was least trustworthy in my books. At least Bres had never lied to me... yet.

"Oh that's right I forgot. Cichol isn't very trustworthy either is he?" He clucked to me. "He tricked you for years!" His laughter filled the room again. It was evil, there was no humour in the sound. He slapped his hands on the table and the plates of food jumped and clattered back down on the table. Cichol didn't budge, this must be a normal occurrence around here, but I jumped back and slid my chair back.

"Don't make me stand up and get you" he said calmly as he continued eating. It was a threat.

Cichol grabbed some food and put it in front of me. "Eat." Again no emotion! I hated him and he was going to pay.

I slid my chair back and took a bite of my roast meat. My eyes nearly rolled back in my head. It took all my will power not to moan out loud - It was good. God it was good. I kept eating.

"Good isn't it?" Bres chuckled.

I nodded my head but choose not to talk. I still couldn't figure this man out yet.

We ate in silence for a while. Bres and Cichol polished off the last of the food. I sat on my little chair unsure of what was going to happen next.

The plates were cleared away and the table taken away. Cichol stood up and walked towards the doorway. He turned and stood guard. My saliva dropped to the back of my throat as I felt a rush of air and a large hand clamp around my throat. I tried kicking my legs at the assault but they just hit air. I was being held up by my throat and I couldn't reach Bres with my arms or my legs, he was too large. He was holding me out as far as he could. My throat burnt and I started to claw at his hand. He didn't budge, I wasn't hurting him. I could feel my face blowing up and flashes of light in my eyes. This was it, this was my death.

Then he dropped me. I landed in a pile on the ground. I grabbed my neck and sucked in as much air as I could. It burned on its way down but it was better than having none at all.

"Remember before when I said I had a problem? Forgive me, I should have said problems - plural. It was true I was hungry, but my other problem is this... you!"

I hung my head still grasping for air. I couldn't respond and I didn't care. I already knew I was the problem.

"You are my number one problem at the moment. You hold the light that's been plaguing me for an eternity." He whined dramatically. "I can smell my ex-wife on you, and it's making me sick. Her light is in you. I want it and I want to extinguish it, burn it out. I want it GONE!" He walked around me in circles. "But therein lays the problem. I could just kill you... but that won't work would it. No, that would mean your light would just go to somebody else."

"What I need to do is to kill you, yes, but as I kill you I need to trap *her* light that is entwined in your body." He stopped and crouched beside me. "Or maybe I could just keep you here for forever, that way I know I have her light and she can't get it. But eventually you will die, because you are human and that's what happens, and then it will all unfold again." He stood up. "What do you think Cichol?" he stopped Cichol answering. "I already know what he wants. He wants you dead!"

I flinched. "Yeah well, I kind of figured that out already."

His evil laughter filled the room. "She speaks, and she is funny. Cichol, you never told me she was funny." Cichol stood still and glared at me.

"What *Cichol* – cat got your tongue?" I teased with sarcasm dripping off my tongue. "Not man enough to answer for yourself?" I could see the veins popping out of his neck. It was working. I was getting under his skin.

Bres watched with amusement. "I do believe Cichol, that she may hate you more than she hates me."

"It would appear that way." Cichol replied between clenched teeth. "If that's all, I'd like to rest now."

Bres waved him away. "Yes of course, go my champion. Rest."

Cichol left without even looking my way. I didn't know what I expected but it hurt. He was leaving me here in this prison and worst of all with Bres, who was so unpredictable he could kill me at any moment. It still didn't seem right. He was the one that I used to phone when I was upset, when I needed a problem solved... he was my Hayden. But not anymore – He was Cichol, the commander of Bres's army of Fomorians.

"You can rest too. I need time to figure out what to do with you." He walked out of the room leaving the table and chairs where they were. He never looked back as the prison door was locked behind him.

CHAPTER 17

I had no idea how long I'd been in this dark and dingy prison for. The days all merged into one. I hadn't seen Hayden, I mean *Cichol* again since our last encounter and quite frankly I didn't want to. I hated him so much I wanted to punch his face in. How dare he betray me... he had been my best friend. Even though I didn't see him, I did see Bres, daily. I cringed whenever I heard his heavy slow footsteps heading towards my prison cell. I never knew what mood he would be in and it terrified me. Would it be nice Bres or evil Bres? Sometimes he'd feed me, sometimes he'd beat me. My body was black and blue and my face was swollen, I couldn't even see out of my left eye from my last beating and for that he gave me no explanation, he just walked through my prison door and kicked me in the stomach, then threw me across the room. I heard a crack as I hit the solid rock wall of my prison. It was my elbow, the pain was intense I nearly passed out. I didn't show him my fear and I don't think that would have mattered, he kept going using me like a punching bag. When he finally left, I crumpled in a heap on the floor. I felt for my elbow and pain shot up my arm and I cried out in pain. Tears rolled down my face. I don't think I'm going to survive this. There was no light where I was being held, and I guaranteed that was on purpose, there was no fire, just damp coldness.

I could draw no light to myself, no flame to defend myself with, no heat to keep me warm. I felt completely lost and beaten.

I thought about my family constantly and hoped they were okay. If they were okay they would be worried about me. I should have been back from Kate's holiday home in Brighton by now. They would have called the police and everyone would be out looking for me. Why did I follow Uar? I should have stayed where I was, and none of this would have happened. I'd be at home, happy and probably still friends with Hayden because he would have still been lying to me and I'd be none the wiser. I was happy, warm and loved there, why did I leave? Uar didn't know where I was, I knew that now. The guards seemed pretty adamant that no one was coming for me. No one knew where Bres's armies were – no one. Somehow I had to get out of this situation by myself and I had no idea how to. I'd hardly eaten anything let along drink anything. My elbow was fractured, I was sure of it. I felt feeble and weak against these Fomorians. I had no more tears left I needed to fight, I needed to find my strength within myself and fight.

Bres had called in a witch called The Crone to help him capture my light. I cringed, that meant my end was near. If they figured out how to capture my light, then I was dead. I had to get out of here. I heard my guards talking about me and the progress of the Crone's work, they didn't seem to care I could hear them and I suppose it made no difference, they knew and I knew I wasn't ever leaving this cell alive.

I heard Bres's familiar footsteps and cringed. God, what mood was he in today? I cradled my elbow. I couldn't stand another beating.

"And how is my favourite guest of honour today?"

I spat at him.

He laughed at me as he opened my prison door. I backed away. "Now now, no need to be like that. I have great news. Wonderful news in fact."

"Yeah, and what's that? You finally fixed your shower so I don't have to smell your stink every time you come for these *friendly* visits."

I regretted it the instant I said it and clenched my teeth. He pinned me with his death stare. I could see a storm brewing in the depths of the dark blue ocean of his eyes. He clenched his fists. I closed my eyes waiting for it, waiting for the punch or kick, whatever punishment tickled his fancy today. But nothing came.

"No matter" he said. I opened my eyes and the storm in his eyes had faded and I was faced with gentle waves. "It doesn't matter my dear Brigid because tomorrow I will be taking the light from you."

I took a sharp intake of breath.

"Yes Brigid, take in the air around you, gulp it down."

My eyes were turning feral, I had to get out of here and out of here now. I knew what he meant, tomorrow I'd be dead.

"You may not get to breath it in for much longer, so please be my guest, suck it up, feel it in your lungs, in your heart. Feel it keeping you alive... for now – Ha ha!" His booming evil laugh filled the room with dread and truth.

My head was spinning. I had to get out of here and it had to be now. He'd turned his back on me while he laughed and why wouldn't he, I was no threat to him, look at him. He was huge and powerful. I was a little girl compared to him. I couldn't even harness my power in this dark stinking prison.

"I have asked the witch to keep you alive, I find you amusing and besides… I need a new slave, but she seems to think that you would not survive the process. I did argue with her for a moment, but then I realised… I didn't really care." He threw his head back and laughed again.

I took my opportunity and jumped on his huge back, I yanked at his long hair and bite the side of his face. I was going for his ear but I couldn't find it through his masses of hair so I clamped down hard on whatever my teeth connected to.

He roared and ripped me off his back. I slid across the cold floor as he came bounding towards me with heavy footsteps. Blood was on his cheek. I hadn't gone too deep, but deep enough to make him bleed. He threw his head forward and head butted me. A wall of black blocked my brain as I heard his evil laughter bounce off the walls as I blacked out.

My head was pounding. I went to put my hands up against my forehead but they wouldn't move. I jerked them roughly forward. Something was holding them back. I tried to open my eyes. I definitely couldn't see out of my left eye now, it had completely swelled over. God I must look a sight at the moment. I cringed as a wave of nausea hit me and I threw up on the floor beside me. Once I got myself sorted and started to think clearly I realised my hands had been bound behind me. He'd tied my hands up – argh! Great, just great. There was no way out this, I was going to die. I had given it my best shot and it wasn't good enough. What was I thinking anyway, as if I could defeat him and even if I could what would I do then, just run out the prison's front doors… I don't think so. I was a goner. But hey, at least I had tried. At least I can die knowing that I'd tried. Oh my god my parents, they are going to be devastated. I'm going to be one of those missing children that never makes it home. They will never know if I'm alive or if I'm dead. This will break them. And what about Uar and the Gold Belts, I'd let them down. I hadn't finished what I'd come here to do, I hadn't released their Mother. They were going to be bound to this broken place forever, enslaved and diseased. And poor Zeg, what was he going to do? Would he go back to my house or would he stay with Uar. I hoped he'd go back home and look after my family for me. Was Zeg even alive? I was broken and bruised, I had no more tears left. I was going to fight to the end, I was not going to make this easy for them. I sat up and swung my legs around to stand up. Great! Bres had my ankles shackled in metal chains. I wasn't going anywhere in a hurry. I looked up as I heard the clink of the lock to my cell.

It was Cichol. At first my heart fluttered with relief, my friend was here, thank god, something familiar. But then I remembered it was all a lie and he was the enemy and wanted me dead. He was the reason why I was here. "Great, to what do I owe this pleasure?" I spat on the ground and saw an outline of blood in my saliva against the grey stone.

He saw it too. He waved the two guards away. "Leave us."

They bowed and walked away, locking us both in.

He walked slowly over to me and knelt down in front of me. I felt ashamed of my pile of vomit and my appearance. I knew he could smell it and I shouldn't care but I did. He touched my forehead gently above my swollen eye. I flinched. "Don't."

"Brig, I'm sorry."

"Ha, sorry - are you kidding me right now." He kept kneeling taking in my appearance. "Yeah take a good look. You did this to me. This is your fault."

"No this is your fault. If you had listened to me you would be back home lying on your safe and cosy bed talking to me on the phone. You would be safe, you would be with me."

"Yeah about that… I remember you telling me that you were my protector?" I raised my eyebrows to emphasise my statement. "What happened Cichol, I believed you. I trusted you. You promised you would let nothing happen to me." I laughed looking down at my appearance, "clearly that hasn't happened."

He frowned and stood up. He gently lifted me off the cold floor. I resisted him but there wasn't much I could do with my hands and legs bound. I jerked as the blood come back in to my left leg. I tried to nudge him with my shoulder but he held me steady. "That still holds true" he whispered before he kissed me. I tried to head butt him and push him away but he held me steady and kept kissing me. I could hear the guards laughing and shouting encouraging disgusting words at us. I tried to bite his tongue but he didn't budge he took the pain and carried on. He held me hard against his body, I couldn't move and then I felt it. I felt his hands unbinding my hands behind my back as he gently shoved something metal in my mouth with his tongue as he continued to kiss me. I stopped resisting.

"Keep going" he whispered quietly between our lips.

I knew what he meant. I was to carry on this show so the guards wouldn't know he was helping me. I started grunting and resisting again.

"That's it Cichol, you show her who's the boss." One of them shouted.

I bit his lip as he finally pulled away. He wiped the blood away with his hand as he released me. I fell on my bum again and did my best to keep the appearance that my hands were still tied behind my back. Easier said than done when you're falling to the ground with your full weight pulling you down. I screamed as my elbow hit the hard ground. The pain was immense. He winked at me as he walked away and locked the door behind him. What just happened?

Once the guards were out of sight and the darkness in my room started to creep in, I knew it was safe to take the piece of metal that Cichol had given me out of my mouth with my unbound hands. It was a key. It was to unlock my legs that had metal bars around them. I still hated him, even though he'd helped me. But how was this to help me I wondered. I wasn't sure where this was all going, but I could feel the warmth of survival flow through my body. I could possibly make it out of here alive after all. I worked at the lock for a good ten minutes. I couldn't get the stupid thing open and then I heard a quiet click. Oh thank god. I looked around to make sure no one heard and when I was certain no one was there, I took them off. I rubbed my sore ankles making sure to keep them close to me if anyone came in. I really hoped Cichol wasn't doing this out of some sick pleasure he may get of giving me hope before it comes crashing down on me. I dreaded what this witch was going to do to me and even if I did survive Bres would keep me. He would beat me and make my life a living hell just for his pure pleasure to see me suffer. I had to get out of this and I was wondering whether Cichol was giving me a fighting chance or whether this was another sick way of making me suffer.

CHAPTER 18

Bres had wandered into my cell as I as sleeping. I woke up to his scary handsome face inches away from mine, smiling wickedly at me.

"Why good morning my little Brigid and how are you feeling today?" I could hear the sarcasm dripping off his words.

I ungracefully tried to anchor myself off the ground pretending everything was still bound where they were supposed to be. I had put the metal cuffs back on but carefully left them unlocked. My hands though were loosely unbound and I made a special effort to keep my back to the wall and my hands behind my back so he didn't notice. "Is that a trick question?"

He looked me up and down. "Your right, it was a trick question, because you truly look terrible." Pain was shooting up my arm from my elbow, I couldn't see out of my eye, my jaw hurt and I had a splitting headache. "But that does not matter, because today is the day. Yes, that's right, today is the day I get rid of my wife forever!" He screamed the last word in my face. I cringed. I had no idea what today was going to hold. Was I getting out of here? Was Cichol going to continue to be an asshole and play mind games with me to the bitter end? I wasn't sure, but I was going to try and get out of this alive. "You don't look very excited Brigid."

"Well that's hard when I can't even move my face."

He smiled "Yes well, that may be the case but I thought it only fitting to give you a good send off, so… what would you like for your breakfast this morning?"

I stared at him dumbfounded. What did I want for breakfast? This man was bat winged crazy! Why would he even care?

"Come now, I'm extending more of my generosity to you. Have I not already been generous to you? I have feed and roofed you for the last month. I have even given you a couple of my guards to keep you safe. Have I not been generous?" I couldn't believe what I was hearing. He was loony tunes! He clicked his fingers and his guards pulled in a table and one chair. "No matter, I have organised a feast for you little girl, one to warm your heart. A last farewell as it may be." He smiled at me and I actually thought it was sincere. Was this me he was talking to or did he think he was talking to his wife. Was there still something there, did he still feel for her? I saw it in his eyes. There was a softness there that I'd never seen before. Was it possible that he once loved her? "Now I know that you are unable to feed yourself" he stated as he looked at my bound limbs, "so I'm going to have one of my guards feed you. You don't mind do you?" He didn't wait for me to answer. He clicked his fingers again and one of the guards came over and roughly picked me up. "GENTLE!" Bres's voice boomed against the walls, power vibrating the little prison cell. He closed his eyes and took a deep breath. "Gentle please, show some respect. This is a big day, Brigid's big day." The guard nodded and loosened his grip. I cried out at the pain in my elbow. I tried desperately to keep the rope around my hands, if it fell off, I was toast. I was gently placed on the chair. "There, now eat little one, enjoy."

I looked at all the food. I wasn't hungry, I actually felt sick. "Are you not joining me?" I asked Bres. I don't even know why I asked, maybe it was because he always did whenever he decided to feed me.

He gently kissed me on the cheek. "No, not today my little one, not today." He said as he walked away with his hands behind his back and his head bowed. It was a strange thing to see such a powerful man seem so small. I had never seen him like this and I was confused. Was this what he used to be like when Brigid and he were still happily married? Was he actually a decent man once? I wasn't sure, but I knew now that there was love once there for his wife, maybe now that the end was near he was finding it hard to come to terms that she'd be gone for forever soon if his witch succeeds.

I turned to my guard when the cell door closed. He tried to shove some oats in my mouth. I wasn't expecting it and choked as he shoved it down my throat. I threw it up on the ground and coughed up the rest. The guard smacked me across the check. I felt the sting, but didn't care. I eyeballed him as a single tear ran down my bruised cheek. "You will eat!" the guard bellowed.

I heard a loud snap as his head turned unnaturally backwards. He slumped to the ground. "YOU WILL GIVE HER RESPECT TODAY!" Bres boomed from behind my cell door.

The other guard rushed in and dragged his friends limp body out. Bres walked away without a second glance. No one else came in to help me. It didn't matter anyway I wasn't hungry. I didn't want to eat anything. I sat there looking at all of the food. My hands were untied, I could eat but what if someone walked in – I just couldn't do it. There was a big bowl of dried meat. I knew I needed energy if I was going to escape and I also knew that I could grab the dried meat chucks with my teeth and eat at least with a little bit of dignity. I snatched a few and took my time chewing on them, savouring their taste. The more I ate, the more I realised how hungry I was, my body must've been in shut down mode and all it needed was some fuel. I decided to eat as much as I could grab with my mouth, but not too much that I felt too full. I didn't want to be sluggish when the time came.

It wasn't long before Cichol came into my cell followed by two guards covered in the familiar grotesque boils and lumps all over them. The red capes draped across their shoulders. Both held spears in their hands and swords strapped to their belts. I swallowed. This was it. Cichol moved towards me with no emotion on his face.

"It is time." He announced emotionless. I tried to move my chair back to get away from him, but he was too quick. He grabbed me and pulled me up from under my arms. I grunted at the pain. He pulled me close against his body so I could stand up. My heart was pounding, god help me!

"No." I cried. "No!" My scream was more urgent as I pulled away.

He kept his hold on me. He was strong. "Wait until the times right" he whispered to me quietly before he threw me up over his shoulder.

What did that mean? When would I know when the time was right? Oh my god! I felt like I was going to wet my pants I was still uncertain Cichol was helping me. I didn't know who he was anymore. I was really hoping he was acting as my friend, I felt like he was, but I didn't trust my instincts anymore.

He carried me out of my cell flanked by the two guards. My stomach hurt as it pounded against his shoulder with each step he took, the dried meat I just demolished threatening to pour out over his back.

I mouthed foul language to the two guards following behind us. One of them smiled at me and a shimmer revealed his true identity, it was Hagrid. My mouth dropped opened in total surprise as the illusion shimmered over the other guard and revealed Gurt. It was only for a split second before they were back to their grotesque disguises again. I was so happy to see them both. I tried not to squeak with excitement. Cichol was really helping me, he must be. Why else and how else were the Gold Belts here. Uar must be here to! My heart lit up with the thought of him. He'd found me. I felt a tap on my leg and something was pushed into my hand before we turned a corner and walked down a long stone corridor. I couldn't see what was in front of me because my head was looking backwards. I heard Cichol talking to another guard in front of us before I heard the strain of a heavy door opening. Cichol's grip tightened on me. I took that as a sign that I needed to play my part. I started to kick, scream and use as much foul language as I could imagine. I continued as I was carried down another corridor. I had no idea where they were taking me or where I was going. Was this even going to work?

"Now" Hagrid said after the doors secured shut behind us.

Gurt smacked Cichol around the head with the blunt end of his spear. Cichol turned and I could hear his growl rumble off the walls. He dropped me as Hagrid pounded him in the head again. He dropped to the ground. I scrambled up knocking the metal clasps from my ankles and pulling my hands free from the rope. I could hear guards come from the direction that we'd just been in, they had heard.

"Run" Hagrid whispered. His cloaking spell was off, they were both themselves again. I suppose if they see me running with them, there was not much use disguising themselves. I took his advice and ran. I followed Hagrid as he pushed his way through the next door into an underwater tunnel. I looked behind me before the door closed. I saw Cichol lying on the ground as guards jumped over him to get us. He wasn't moving. I hoped he was going to be okay.

"Keep going!" Gurt yelled. He was behind me pushing me along. I was not the fastest with my injuries and I needed to scream. I ran with all my might. Nausea shot up through my throat. I swallowed it back down and kept going. This was not going to break me.

"Shoot! Keep going I'll hold them off!" Hagrid yelled. I turned to see a wall of guards pushing to get through the door to the tunnel.

"Your hand" Gurt yelled at me as he pushed me forward.

I looked, it was a box of matches. Oh my god, I could help. Without thinking I stopped and lit a match. I flung it forward towards the guards, closed my eyes and pushed my power towards it, I felt the familiar glow roll down my arm and savoured the feeling. *I have missed you* I whispered to my inner self. I looked at the giant wall of fire I'd created in the underwater tunnel. No one was getting through that.

"Good work girlie, now get to the other side."

I high tailed it down the tunnel, feeling the heat of my fire on our backs. I could hear yelling and frustration as we fled further down. My fire wall was holding them all at bay. Fish were swimming above us. I could see them all. This tunnel was an incredibly long wall of glass, or some sort of energy pushing the water out, it was truly amazing. Which made me wonder where the hell I'd been living for the last month? Had I been living under the sea?

I could see someone running towards us from the other end of the tunnel. I stopped. Hagrid bumped into me. "Keep going!"

It was Uar! "Uar!" I screamed and started running faster. I needed him, I needed to feel safe, he was here! He'd found me. There were other people behind him, but I headed straight for him.

He stopped in his tracks and his face drained of colour. I stopped and turned behind me to see what he was looking at. Bres's huge form was walking towards us. He'd grown twice his normal size and was walking through the wall of fire. He didn't flinch as his clothes started to burn. He just grew bigger. I turned and ran with all my might, as Uar ran urgently towards me. I could taste the fear in his eyes.

"NO!" Uar screamed.

I felt a rush of power against my back as it pushed me forward. A huge weight pounded on top of me and I couldn't breathe. The tunnel had collapsed. Water pushed and pulled me in all directions. I saw Bres with his fist pounded into the ground smiling up at me with Cichol flanking his back. He stared at me emotionless as I felt my body being pulled in all directions as the water crashed down around us. I felt arms pull me closer towards a body I hung on for dare life, not knowing if I was hanging onto a friendly person or an enemy, all I knew was that I was hanging on to life, even if it could be for a short time. I felt a pop in my ears as oxygen filled my lungs again. I was still under water, but in a pocket of air.

"Breathe!" Uar yelled as he pulled me closer. He was pulling me away from the carnage. "Breathe, you're safe now, I have you."

I took in deep breaths as I watched the water push past me with great speed. How was Uar doing this? I concentrated on breathing and staying alive. The pocket of air wasn't that big and I was afraid to move or talk in case a handful of sea water filled my lungs.

I silently watched as he pushed me through the murky sea waters. Thanking my lucky stars that he was here and I was safe. He held me tightly against his body and we rushed though the depths of the sea to safety. I had no idea how he was doing this or even more importantly that I'd been in prison under the sea for a month. Crazy, there was no way I knew that I was under water that whole entire time. My life was a whole lot of crazy right now.

As we got to the shore line I could see shadows of large tree branches overhanging the water. I saw a body reaching down with their arms to pull me up. Uar pushed me upwards with his unnatural strength and I protested. He didn't know about my elbow. Too late, those arms latched onto mine and pulled me up. The pain was so intense I screamed and passed out. I must've only passed out for a few minutes because as I woke up I felt my body being passed down a row of people to the safety of dry land through the tangled web of branches that fell so low they dusted the shore lines. I saw a familiar face as she pulled me against her and gave me the biggest hug.

"I'm going to kill the bastard that did this to you." It was Brea, she held me tight and rocked me.

I cried. I didn't care who saw I cried. I cried for my live, I cried for my torture, I cried for their lives, the people that risked theirs to save mine and most importantly I cried for my long-lost friendship with Hayden. He'd helped me and even though he had lied to me, I generally believed he was trying to keep me safe. Maybe he was keeping his promise after all.

"Brigid!" Uar grabbed me out of Brea's arms and rocked me. I felt a familiar weight land on my shoulder and knew instantly it was Zeg. Oh, thank god he was safe. He pulled my earlobe gently so I'd know it was him.

"Zeg" I simply said. "I'm so happy you're safe."

Uar kissed me quickly on the lips as he pulled me in for a tighter hug. "Brigid, I thought I had lost you!" He kept rocking me. I closed my eyes. I could feel a circle of people around us as we lay in a heap in the ground, a human, a god and a little brownie just happy to be together and happy to be alive.

"We need to move" a voice said from within the circle, breaking our solitude.

"Brigid, we need to go." Uar whispered in my ear. I leaned closer towards him and nodded my head. He grabbed me from under my legs and lifted me up. Zeg had tucked himself against my neck and he wasn't letting go. I savoured the feeling of him needing me, it was a good feeling and I was so happy he was safe. Uar started to run after the rest of the group and the stabbing pain ran up my arm again.

"My arm" I yelled. "Put me down, I'm fine, I can run."

He paused but put me down. He looked at me briefly before giving me a gentle shove to keep me moving. I appreciated the fact that he let me run, he let me do what I wanted. He knew that I was capable of getting out of this. So I ran. Zeg held on tighter and I ran quickly behind them. I cradled my arm with the fractured elbow to my side which seemed to help and I drew in the warmth of the sun as we made it out of the branches that guarded us from our enemies. It tingled through my body and I could feel it's strength. Energy was running back through my body, it was like my body was being drained while I was a prisoner and now it was living again. I picked up the pace and caught up with Uar.

Tunnan ran up beside us. He smiled at me as he passed me his smaller bow. "Here, you may need this."

I smiled as I took it from his hand and swung it over my shoulder. He handed me a handful of arrows which I carried in my hand as I ran. He winked at me as he picked up the pace and I kept in line with Uar.

"Incoming!" Brea called as we all hit the deck.

Uar covered me with his shield as arrows showered down on us. I could hear their thuds and the impact as Uar held his shield steady over us. Once the wave was over I leaned out and got my bow and arrow ready. Fomorians were running towards us. Two hit the ground as Tunnan's arrow's hit their mark. I released mine, seeing my target go down I reached for another. They were getting closer. Uar pointed towards a tree with large full branches. I nodded my head as he grabbed me and hoisted me up into its branches. Injuries were now forgotten, I was in my element, I was running on pure adrenalin. Tunnan threw me some more arrows and I added them to my bunch I already had. I climbed up higher, amongst the branches out of sight. I found the position I wanted as Zeg climbed up into my hair. I pulled my bow string to my anchor at the side of my mouth and released, over and over again, each one hitting their mark. Amongst the chaos, no one could see me, they didn't even know what was going on, but one by one they dropped until there was none. I closed my eyes. I had one arrow left. I slowly climbed down the tree. Now that the adrenalin had stopped my body hurt like hell. My eye was still swollen, my head hurt and my elbow was killing me. I literally fell out of the tree on the last branch as Uar caught me. This time he gently put me on the ground but I protested. I didn't think I could walk anymore. I needed to heal. He lifted me up and started walking and I passed out again.

CHAPTER 19

The mattress was soft as I snuggled in further. I heard a familiar snort and knew instantly that Zeg was beside me. I rolled over gently to see a little bum high up the in the air with his knees tucked close to his chest as he snored beside me on my pillow, dribble coming out of his mouth leaving a small wet patch. As usual I pulled the bed covers up over him and gave him a little hug. He grunted and rolled over to his side. I smiled as I turned to stare at the ceiling. I was obviously safe. I'd woken in a comfortable bed with Zeg beside me. There was a door that didn't have guards watching me, I was safe wasn't I? I had a little bit of doubt as my legs swung over the side of the bed. I didn't recognise the room but it looked friendly. It wasn't cold damp rock that I'd been surrounded by for weeks, there was light in here, it wasn't very bright, but I could feel it. I knew it must've been the day time, which would explain why Zeg was sleeping. A pain shot up my arm again. It wasn't as bad as what it had been, but it was still there.

There was a knock at the door.

"Who is it?" I asked sheepishly, feeling ridiculous for asking the question.

"It's me, Uar."

My head fell back in relief. "Come in!" I nearly screamed it out. "I mean, come in" calming my nerves a little bit so I didn't sound so desperate.

The door opened slightly as Uar's head peaked through. "How are you feeling?"

"Like crap" I replied.

He stepped through the door with a plate of food and a cup of something to drink. "Here this will make you feel better, eat and drink." He sat beside me on the bed and handed me the drink first. I took a sip. It wasn't water, it was mead. I shook my head at the sweetness. "It will help."

I smiled and took another gulp, he was right it was helping. I could feel its warmth run through my body, giving me strength. Once I'd finished my cup I turned to him and thanked him. "Thanks for finding me."

He hugged me and kissed me on the forehead. "I was so worried about you. I thought I had lost you forever."

I hugged him tighter as he leaned in and kissed me on the lips. I pulled back a little surprised and he let me go. "I'm sorry, I shouldn't have done that."

I looked at him and realised I needed him. "Yes you should have." I pulled him against me and kissed him. He relaxed in my arms as his tongue reached into my mouth. I savoured it's warmth and matched his urgency. My head started to spin as his tongue reached deeper, needing to feel my response, I responded the same. Our breathing became heavier and I could feel a glowing pulse between us, lighting up the room. I knew I needed him and he needed me. Our glow mingled and danced with each other as our kiss grew with more urgency. A loud snort filled the room and I remembered Zeg. I pulled away and pointed towards the little brownie. Uar looked to where I was pointing. Zeg scratched his bum and rolled over. We both laughed as we fell back on the bed together. We intertwined our hands and lay beside each other in silence. Each knowing we were happy and that this moment was perfect and how it was meant to be. I quickly fell asleep again and woke a few hours later with Uar's arm draped over my hip. I was happy, he'd found me and I was alive and I was with him.

His eyes opened up as he pulled my hips closer toward his belly and I snuggled in closer. I sighed a sigh of happiness and felt the love run through my body. Then I remembered what I must look like. I sat bolt upright. Oh my god! I must look terrible. I'd been beaten until I was black and blue, my eye was closed over, my face swollen… oh no I wanted to crawl into a hole and die. Everyone had seen me like that and I must have stunk. I hadn't had a bath or a shower for a whole month while I was being held prisoner. I must've been covered in my own vomit and blood, not a pretty sight. I looked down at my clothes. I was in a soft white full length nighty. I didn't look dirty. I sniffed under my arms, nothing. I smelt clean. Someone must have cleaned me! I cringed even more, oh no, who cleaned me and more importantly looked at me naked.

"Relax."

I turned to Uar who was now sitting up leaning against his hand. "Did you do this?"

"Do what?"

"Clean me up?"

"Well, Brea gave you a bath, but I helped with some of your bruising."

I breathed a sigh of relief. I must've stunk and I would have been mortified if Uar had done that for me. I needed to thank Brea for doing it, because it would not have been a pretty task. I stood up and looked at my arms. A lot of the bruising had gone down but I still felt immense pain in my elbow. "My elbow is still killing me, I think he fractured it."

"He. You mean my father did this to you?"

"Yes Uar, your father did this to me when he threw me up against that bloody stone wall."

He sat up and bowed his head. "I'm sorry Brigid that he did that to you."

"He did more things to me than that Uar, he tortured me every day. I was beaten and abused continuously." Anger brewed up in me as I clenched my fists when the memories of what I'd endured came back up to the surface. "Every day I would cringe when I heard his footsteps heading towards my cell." I started crying. Uar got out of bed and pulled me towards him. There was a fire lit and he gently lifted me towards it and sat me down on his knee. I felt the warmth of the fire warm my broken soul and I poured my heart out to Uar. I told him everything that had happened, every little detail that I could remember and knew about. Even about Cichol kissing me and pushing that key into my mouth.

Once I'd finished he was silent. He nuzzled his head into my neck as I cried. He stayed silent and let me have my moment. There were a lot of things that I didn't understand and it frustrated me.

"What's going on Uar? I'm so confused. Cichol helped me, I thought he wanted to kill me and we just left him there. What is going to happen to him?"

Uar pushed me gently away from him so I could look at him in the eyes. "When you were captured. Zeg was with you. He hid away in your armour. Cichol and his army took you under the sea to Bres, my father." He choked slightly as he said the word father. "Zeg stayed with you until he knew where you were going to be held then he teleported to me to tell me where you were."

"He can do that?"

"Yes that is part of his abilities as a brownie, but he has to know where he is going and be connected to somebody to get there."

"Wow, I had wondered what had happened to him. But if you knew where I was, why didn't you come sooner?" I remembered the nights sitting on the cold hard ground wondering if Uar was ever going to find me, whether he'd save me. That was before I realised, I needed to toughen up and get on with figuring out how to get myself out.

"We did. We marched an army to where Zeg said you were, once we got to the spot Bres was no longer there. That's when we realised Bres must be constantly on the move."

"What? I was never moved. I stayed exactly where I was, in my cold stinking hole of a prison room."

"No you wouldn't have felt it. Bres is very powerful and his encampment under the sea must be enchanted, it moves every two days and only Bres and his general know the coordinates."

"Cichol."

"Yes Cichol and Bres."

Realisation hit me. "Cichol told you where I was going to be didn't he."

Uar nodded. "I must admit when he first showed up I wanted to cut his head off, but that was until I felt his commitment to you and I knew in spite of everything he was trying to keep you safe, so I listened to him... after Brea tried to drown him." A smile grew on his face as the satisfied moment of Brea trying to drown Cichol replayed itself in his mind. "But, he is a hard man to kill your... friend."

I cringed at the mention of the word friend. Was he still my friend? I had hated him and wished him dead so many times in my prison cell, after all he was the reason I was there, but then he did something that I did not expect – he helped me live. "Yeah, I suppose he is a friend." I bowed my head as a tear slid down my cheek.

Uar licked it away with his tongue. Shivers ran through my body and we kissed again. His hand massaged my thigh as the kiss deepened.

"Brigid!"

We quickly pulled away as the door swung open and banged against the wall as Hagrid walked in. He had a big smile on his face and if he'd seen us kissing he didn't say anything. He walked quickly over to me and lifted me off Uar's lap and trapped me in a huge bear hug, spinning me around in circles. "Brigid, Brigid, Brigid boy am I happy to see you!" He laughed. "I thought you were a goner when we couldn't find ya." He spun me one last time before placing me gently on the ground.

"Hagrid." I started to cry again. Dam it, what was I crying for. I was all emotional. "Hagrid... thank you."

He pulled me into a hug again. "No, no, no more tears. You are safe and you are welcome."

"Thank you, I owe you big time." I turned away and wiped my eyes.

I looked at Uar. He was still sitting on the seat, and Zeg was sitting on his shoulder, both had huge goofy smiles on their faces. Zeg stood up and blew me a kiss. I squeezed his cheek gently with my thumb and index finger as he shyed away, embarrassed at the attention. I giggled as I sat back down on Uar's knee.

Hagrid smiled as he looked at us both. He didn't say anything, he just nodded at Uar and Uar nodded back. That must be some sort of man code for something us girls don't know about.

Uar kissed me on the forehead as I leaned back into him. His muscles relaxed as I tucked in against his chest. I felt the bulges of his muscles as I wriggled, trying to get comfortable. "So, what now?" Hagrid asked.

Uar sighed and looked at me and surveyed my face. "First of all we have to fix this wee one."

"Agreed." Hagrid said. "Have you had a good look at yourself yet" he smiled as he asked me, but I wasn't sure if it was in good humour or if he was wondering if I had or not. And I hadn't, I had no idea what I looked like. I actually didn't want to know.

"No, I haven't looked, I don't want to either. Just heal me Uar, please, I'm not interested to see what that beast did to me. I just want it erased from me."

Uar and Hagrid looked at each other, another silent secret man code thing. I huffed. "Okay, let's do this. Uar, what's the best way to do this." I knew that Uar had healed a lot of my injuries, but he wasn't strong enough unless he was with me to fully heal me.

"Let's go outside."

"What outside where everyone can see?" Was he mad. "I thought we were in hiding. Don't we have a whole army after us?"

"Well yes we do, but..." he smiled. "Come and see for yourself."

He took my hand as he helped me through the door. I winced at the pull on my elbow and swapped hands with him. He apologised as we walked down a thin hallway. Where were we? I had no idea where we were and I hadn't even asked the question yet. I was just so happy to be safe and alive and with my dream man, that I don't think I really cared. I felt safe and that is what mattered. The hall had open windows, more like archways opening up the side of the walls. The sun streamed down to my fingers. "The sun!" I blurted out. Uar gave me a massive smile. "The sun is out, I thought the sun never came out here anymore... Are we still in the Otherworld, your world" I asked Uar.

He nodded his head. "Yes Brigid we are."

"Wow, I never realised how beautiful it was." I looked through one of the archways and stopped. I walked up to it and put my hand on the peach coloured stone and closed my eyes. The warmth was one of the best feelings I'd felt in a long time. I hadn't seen any sun while I was under the sea. This moment I was locking away in my memory forever. I heard familiar clinks and clanks as I looked down below into an open grass courtyard, fully enclosed by a large peach coloured wall. Brea waved at me as she noticed me leaning over the window. There were a few of the Gold Belts training. They all stopped and looked up at me with big smiles on their faces. I smiled back as we made our way down to them.

CHAPTER 20

There was an old stone well that stood a metre above the ground in the middle of the courtyard. Uar stopped me once we reached it. Everyone came closer to us, nodding their well wishes to me. I thanked them all for helping me one by one as we passed. I appreciated that they had put their own lives at risk to safe mine. I knew I was important to them and the key to finishing their curse, but they didn't have to risk their own lives, but they still did. It was more than I could ever ask of them.

I looked frantically around for Gurt, only now realising that I hadn't seen him yet since the tunnel caved in around us under the sea. "Gurt?" I yelled out. I looked frantically at Uar. "Where's Gurt? I haven't seen him yet."

He frowned not saying anything.

"Where's Gurt Uar?"

"He didn't make it back."

"What?" Oh my god, Gurt. What have I done. I felt like vomiting. I leaned up against the well. "This is all my fault."

Familiar warm arms wrapped around me and pulled me in. "No, this is not your fault. This is my father's fault. Besides, we sent a small group of Gold Belts out to search for Gurt. He'll be fine… it's Gurt. We will find him."

He kissed my forehead. "I hope so, I don't know if I could stand it if he lost his life to save mine."

"He'll be fine. They will find him Brigid."

I certainly hope so. He could be injured somewhere, lying in hiding dying somewhere. Oh, the guilt was overwhelming.

"Ready?" Uar asked.

I looked into the well and nodded my head. I was ready to get the memories removed permanently from my body. They would be forever in my mind, but at least I wouldn't have to look at them every day in the mirror. I stared at the dark water below. I sensed the ripples before I could see them. Strands of bright copper hair swirled, rippling the water. Brigid, their Mother was here.

I turned to Uar. He nodded his head and smiled. He knew, he could see her too. We both leaned over and starred lovingly into the water. I felt the light from Uar enter my body, it was so intense I closed my eyes and let his healing powers heal me physically. It was euphoric, it was intense and very very welcomed. I felt the pressure leave my eye socket as the swelling disappeared. My elbow was next as I felt a small pop. I opened my eyes in surprise and rubbed my elbow. Nothing, it didn't hurt anymore. I felt strong and very empowered. I felt like a new woman.

"Thanks Uar" I pulled him in close and hugged him.

From over his shoulder I could see the Gold Belts kneeling on the grass in front of us. Their eyes and mouths wide open. I had seen this before when Uar first healed me. It must've still taken them by surprise. There was a huge light last time as our light combined as one to heal me. But this time they look absolutely gobsmacked.

"Well I'll be" Tunnan whispered from the crowd loud enough for me to hear him.

"What?" Even Uar was looking at me strangely. "What? What's happened? Did it not work?"

"Ah, you may want to look at your hair." I heard Brea say beside me as she gently flicked a lock of it over my shoulder.

OMG! My hair had turned orange. Not just any orange, it glowed. "What?" I pulled all my hair over my shoulder and ran my hands urgently through it willing it to turn back to blond. "How can this be?" My hair shimmered with rays of light weaving in and out of its silky long copper locks. It was like Brigid the goddess's hair. I have her hair. She gave me her hair.

"I have her hair!" I yelled out to everyone. They all just stared back at me astonished.

I turned to Uar. "She gave me her hair."

He too looked astonished as he took a step towards me and gently ran his fingers through it.

"Why would she do that?" I whispered.

I felt an object shooting towards me, the shadow just about hitting my face. I threw my arm out to block whatever was going to hit me. A fiery arrow hit the rock before it hit my face and split it in half.

"That's why" Tunnan said as he strolled out of the crowd juggling a couple of rocks casually in his hands.

I stared at him. "You threw a rock at me?" I yelled astonished that he'd do that. "You threw a rock at me!" I yelled again as another fiery arrow flew out of my hand, barely missing his smug face.

"Yes and lucky you have bad aim."

I threw another one at him. This time it landed on the ground in between his feet. "How do you know I was aiming at you."

I heard sniggering amongst the crowd as Tunnan took a step back.

"Enough!" Uar shouted. He took my hands in his and turned them over. He gently wiped his fingers over the palm of my hand where the faint glowing line of an arrow marked it. "She has given you her fire arrow."

"Her arrow? You mean that fire thing that keeps coming out of my hand."

He nodded.

I was confused. How was this even possible. "I'm confused. She can do that?"

He nodded again.

"What does it all mean?" I asked as I turned my hands over looking at the mark on my hand.

"I think Mother has given you a helping hand so to speak. With that arrow, we may just have a fighting chance." He turned to the Gold Belts who were now standing up. "We have a chance!" He yelled. "Our Mother will be coming home to us!"

The group roared into cheers as Uar stood in front of them with his hands on his hips in a Peter Pan stance and a smile like the Cheshire Cat. I gulped.

Tunnan stood in front of me. We both held long wooden fighting staffs. Uar and Brea were to the side of us. I took my fighting stance as Uar had showed me waiting for Tunnan to make his first move. He stepped forward and brought his stick down in front of me, I stood still. I knew he was going to do that, he wanted to see what my reaction was going to be. Would I flinch. He gave me a cheeky smile and stood back where he was before. Before he could react I quickly jabbed my staff into his stomach. He attacked by swinging his staff forward, as I blocked the hit to my head. I could hear words of encouragement from Brea as we fought together. Uar was standing silent, watching us with his arms crossed over his bare chest. You see, now that I had the fire arrow inside me, I felt invigorated. I felt different. I could sense things before they happened and I was strong. I lot stronger than before. My aim was intense. Long distance I still hit my target. My senses were being overwhelmed and I was loving it. Tunnan struck his staff down on mine before he flipped it over to knock my staff out of my hand. He failed, before it could I pulled back and swept the ground taking his legs out behind him. I stood over him with a huge smirk.

"Ha, I have you now" I gloated.

He swung his leg around and took me down with him. He leap to his feet from his back and held the staff at my throat. "You were saying?" Bugger! I grimaced as he held his hand out to help me up. He yanked as I came to my feet. "Never assume you've won until they are dead."

He was right, I was getting too cocky. This power was making me feel invincible and as Tunnan had just shown me, I certainly was not. I need to remember that.

The Gold Belts had started testing me, training me, seeing what I was capable of now that I had this fire arrow gifted to me by the lady of the sacred flame. We all knew I could aim and was good with a bow and arrow, but I also now had strength and intuition and did I mention my fighting skills. I was like a black belt ninja… well maybe not that extreme, but it was just as excellent.

I found out we were currently staying at Aberline Castle, Tunnan's house, well his parent's old house before they were killed. It wasn't the sort of house I imagined Tunnan to live in or grow up in, it was very grand. He didn't look like the *grand* type. It was more like a fortified villa than a castle. It was huge and secluded with two stories of peach coloured stone. It had exposed archways as the wings of the house met each other. It semi circled around a large courtyard with a stone well in the middle. It was surrounded by a tall stone fortified fence. It was so thick that the Gold Belts could walk on the top of it while they patrolled the surroundings by the villa. They were guarded by a taller layer of stone on the outer side with slits strategically placed. I kind of imagined him living in some sort of stick hut, or maybe a cave out in the woods somewhere, away from people, like a hermit. I really wanted to know a bit more about him, he was shrouded in mystery. He didn't live here, in this house, instead he chose to live as a nomad, constantly moving from place to place. Hunting his food and bartering meat and animal skins for items he needed. I could feel the pain it caused him even being here in this house. It must be filled with bad memories for him.

There was a caretaker that would come by once a week to check on things, but other than that the house was left on its own with no one to love it. It was kind of sad. The house was naked and bare, no pictures, minimal furniture, the house was left unloved. It was a shame because I could imagine back in its day it would have been amazing.

One-night Tunnan had gone to bed early and I finally managed to hear part of his story over a warm fire with our bellies filled with food and mead. I was sitting on Uar's knee as Hagrid told the story. Tunnan's family were on Bres's side of the fight when he was betrayed and taken down by the people he ruthlessly ruled over. Tunnan's Mother Adela, lured Brigid away to the cliff to show her a flower, the ghost orchid. *I was told the real name of the ghost orchid but it was too weird, it went in one ear and out the other… I was just going with the name ghost orchid for now, that one I could remember.* Apparently it was really rare and depended on some sort of fungus to make it grow, and Adela had told Brigid that she'd seen it bloom over by the cliffs when she was collecting wild garlic. Brigid was desperate to see it, Adela knew this and showed her where she *saw* it. Brigid knew something was wrong as she walked closer to the cliff. She looked into Adela's soul and saw betrayal on Adela's aura, but it was too late. Brigid trusted Adela, she was one of her closest friends. Adela smiled at her as Bres froze her. Brigid whispered silent words as the stone immobilised her and covered her body in stone. Three shots of light flew out of her mouth before it was covered forever with stone. One hit Adela and she fell down dead. One went to Bres, but he managed to dodge it and the other flew up high into the sky. The look of despair and betrayal could still be seen on her face captured in stone for eternity. Tunnan's father, Herman was devastated by the death of his beloved wife, but still remained faithful to Bres and carried on as a commander of his army, before he mysteriously disappeared. No one has heard from him since. Adela's betrayal of Brigid and his father's disappearance has been eating Tunnan up ever since. He acknowledges his family was on the wrong side of the fight but he'll claim allegiance with no one. He was a free spirit anchored down by no one or no side. He was with us because he believed it was the right thing to do and maybe in some way it might heal the pain in his soul from his family's betrayal of our Mother of the sacred flame.

I went to bed that night thinking of Tunnan. He made a bit more sense to me now. He'd no control over his family's actions, just as he had no control over Bres freezing Brigid, but I bet the guilt was eating him up inside. No wonder he stayed away from people. If his parents were capable of that sort of betrayal what could other people do to him or to the people he loved. I felt sorry for him. I knew he wouldn't appreciate it if I talked to him about it, so I was going to leave it where it was and just carry on pretending that I didn't know the truth, but I'd carry on with a lot more respect for Tunnan than I was currently giving him. I tucked Uar's warm strong arm around my belly as I felt the pull of sleep take hold of me.

CHAPTER 21

"We have to do something" Brea said, "and we need to move soon."

Uar agreed. "I agree, the sun is out but our Mother is not. Bres will be planning and we need to be one step ahead of him." Uar cringed with the mention of his father's name.

Uar had called a meeting with all the heads of the Gold Belts and me, I was invited too. Zeg was sitting on my shoulder looking on anxiously.

"If the front entrance to Brigid is blocked, then why don't we just take the back way?" I asked curiously. Surely there's another way to her, if there was a front, there must be a back."

"Good idea Brigid except the back is blocked too. The bones of judgement only allow entrance from the front. Our Mother made sure that was the only way through before she froze." Yute said looking glum.

"Well... there is Grisbid rock." Hagrid mumbled.

I heard Brea snort. "Grisbid rock is a tall thin hunk of rock about two miles from the back of the cliff, surrounded by deep sea." Brea said. "There is no way we can get to the cliffs from there and even if we could, we wouldn't get through."

"Yes but it looks directly to the back of the cliff, that can't be a coincidence." Hagrid replied.

"I agree" Brea said, "but we've been there, it's baron and near impossible to climb. I don't see how there's any connection."

"Did you say Grisbid?" I asked.

"Yes Grisbid rock" Brea answered.

"How do you spell it?"

"Why?"

I think I was onto something. "Just, how do you spell it?"

"G.R.I.S.B.I.D" Brea said slowly. She didn't believe there was any connection between this rock and the cliff.

The whole room was silent. The wheels in my mind were running full speed. "Has this rock always been there?"

"Well, no. It actually only appeared the day our Mother was frozen."

"Ah ha!" I yelled as I jumped up. Zeg jumped onto Uar's shoulder as I marched around. "I know what to do!" I paced eagerly around the room with enthusiasm. "If the rock appeared the day Brigid froze, it must be a clue, something to help us get across another way."

"Yes but we've been there. I've climbed it and it's impossible, it seems to have no connection except for when it appeared. We can't swim across the channel separating the rock and the cliff face. There's a beast that lives far below and even if we climb the cliff, we can't get through the barrier, I've tried. The bones of judgement are the only way through."

"That maybe so, but you've never had me before."

"What do you mean?" Brea asked.

"Grisbid rock!" I yelled again slower.

I felt Uar wrap his arm around me. "You are a genius."

I turned and kissed him on the lips. "Yes I am. Do you not get it? Did you never do wordplays at school?"

Everyone looked at me strangely. "Yes word plays. It's when you try to make a word out of jumbled letters and Grisbid rock unjumbles to Brigid's rock."

The room fell silent again before everyone started talking excitedly to each other, the penny dropped. "You see it has to have something to do with it. There must be a way, and maybe you never saw it before because I wasn't here."

Brea fell silent and looked into the fire. "Yes" she murmured. "Maybe you're right." I could see her thinking in her mind, letting the information sink in.

"We need to go there. You need to show me where it is." I knew once I was there I'd know what to do. I didn't know what it was yet, but I knew deep down inside myself that this is what has to happen. This was the way.

"I agree with Brigid, we need to take her to the rock." Uar said. "We will get you up to the top and guard you while you figure out what it is we are to do from there."

"Yes, we'll figure it out." Brea said. "Right, you all know what to do. We leave at daylight."

Everyone made their way to their beds, except Tunnan. He stood to the side of the doorway shrouded in darkness. "Are you coming with us?" I asked gently.

He didn't answer but looked away. Uar pushed me through the door gently and whispered "I'll join you soon."

I looked between Tunnan and him. "Fine" I huffed. "I'll see you soon." It was clear Uar wanted to talk with Tunnan and quite frankly he could talk to him for as long as he wanted. I needed my bed. It was going to be a big day tomorrow. Tomorrow was going to be my awakening, and I hoped I wasn't leading anyone astray and that I really would know what to do once we got there. This was our only option, there were no more. We definitely couldn't get through the bones of judgement anymore, the Fomorians wouldn't let that mistake happen again. This rock was the key, I knew it was, it had to be.

We set out at first light. I'd put on some leather pants and golden chest armour. My hair was piled high on top of my head gathered into a pony tail. A trail of glowing light fell down my back. I rubbed the fire arrow on my palm and smiled. I'll meet you soon. I had a sword strapped to my belt and Tunnan's small bow and arrow strapped to my back, not that I needed it anymore since I could shoot fire arrows from my hands, which was very cool, but I liked the feel of the bow and arrow on my back. It strangely gave me reassurance and strength remembering what I'd been through and what I'd done and survived. Zeg had made himself at home in a small leather coin purse Uar gave me that I'd strapped onto my belt. He looked happy he was coming with us and I wouldn't have it any other way.

It took us a couple of days to get to Black's bay where we needed to be to get to Grisbid Rock. We took the long way around so as not to draw attention to ourselves. We didn't want to give Bres and his merry band of Fomorians a heads up. It was a long couple of days which gave me time to think and my mind filled of thoughts of my family. They must be worried like crazy. I missed them, I even missed Tom. I couldn't wait to see them and if all this worked out, that could be soon. I'd be seeing them soon. How I was going to explain my disappearance was beyond me. Was I going to tell them the truth, would they even believe me or was it best I lied. Maybe this was something I should speak to Uar about. I didn't know if there was some sort of *God* code that you weren't allowed to talk about it… kind of like fight club. The first rule of fight club - you don't talk about fight club.

Zeg's powers surprised me daily. He's teleporting skills were unreal! He was so small, so to get anywhere quickly, like stealing Hagrid's food for instance, he'd teleport to grab the food and back to me again. It was utterly hilarious. He'd look up at me with a cheeky smug grin. I would give him a wee tickle on the back and a giggle. He'd rock back and forth on his little bum silently laughing as Hagrid sat by the fire seething. Hagrid knew he couldn't catch Zeg, how could he – Zeg could teleport as quickly as he could blink.

My hair whipped around my face in the wind as I looked out to Grisbid Rock. It was about ten metres in diameter, not very wide at all, but what it lacked for in width it made up for it in height. It stood straight out from the sea, about ten stories above the sea level. It was a sight I'd never seen before, it certainly didn't look natural. This rock was put here for a reason and I was going to figure out why. The rock sat out in the middle of Black's Bay so we had to take a row boat out to it. We had come across a few Fomorians on the way here, but hid from them, rather than risk being seen. We saw none around Black's Bay though.

Brea reckoned that was because there was no way to get in through the back and Bres knew it. He was keeping all his cavalry to the front, where the attack should be coming from. The water was dark and cold. I could see shadows ducking and diving out of sight. Large dark murky colours, giving me the hebe-gebes. I wasn't sure if I was seeing things or not. Maybe my mind was playing tricks on me like when I was a child and I used to think monsters were hiding in my closet if it was slightly open. My parents had to shut it for me so I'd sleep.

"Ahhh, is this safe?" I asked nervously as I looked into the dark depths of the ocean. I was in the small wooden row boat with Uar and some of the other Gold Belts. Zeg had taken his place upon Uar's shoulder. Standing tall looking into the distance like he was waiting for something. Brea was in a back-up boat with Tunnan and some others following closely behind. The rest stayed hidden on the beach. Not all of us could get over. There were only a limited number of row boats and limited room on top of the rock.

"Yes, you're fine. The water is deep here that's all." Uar answered, but I saw him gulp as he looked into the depths. He was scared too. Were there monsters in the bottom of this sea?

We continued on, dodging small swells of the sea until we got to the cliff face of Grisbid Rock. There was nowhere to park up, no beach or stony edge, it was a sheer cliff face. How were we going to get up this? I looked up the length of the rock, my head falling back as far it could go. Jeez, this was not going to be easy. We slowly made our way around to the back side of it, the side furthest away from the cliff face that held the lady of the sacred flame. Uar jumped out onto a small flat surface, Zeg held on for dear life at the impact. I could hear Uar's sword clang against his shield when he landed. He stood there like a living god, which I supposed he kind of was. The size of him and his presence was magnificent, I was falling in love with this guy, actually I think that was too late, I was already in love with this guy, from the first moment I saw him in my dreams. He reached down for me to follow him. He pointed to small holes that had been etched out of the rock. It looked like a crude type of ladder, something we could use to climb it.

"We have to climb that?"

Uar nodded as I landed neatly beside him.

"Well, at least there are foot holes… that's good, right?" That had to make things easier surely.

"Up you go" Uar said as he bowed in front of me. "Ladies first."

"Ladies first my ass" I mumbled to myself as I put my foot in the first foot hole and my hand above it.

"What?"

"Nothing, I said nothing. Let's get this over and done with." I called back as I started to climb. Uar had a smile on his face as he and Zeg followed closely behind.

One by one we started to climb, one behind the other like little ducklings following their mother. I'd hate to lose my footing and slip, knocking everyone down like dominos. That would suck.

The higher we got the windier it got. My hair kept getting in my eyes, even though it was tied up. The glowing orange kept catching my eye and distracting me, I was still unused to the blinding glowing colour. Every time it would hit my face I'd expect it to be blond. I cursed as I kept climbing. I was getting to a point where I didn't want to look down, I couldn't look down. Instead I looked up, I was close to the top, not too much further to go. My muscles ached and were starting to shake. This was hard work, I truly hoped I knew what to do once I got up there. I managed to drag myself over the top to the flat grassy top. I crawled to the middle, to the safest place and lay on my back and breathed. I closed my eyes and kept breathing letting my muscles recover. Everyone did the same. Uar was beside me and passed me his water. I gulped it back greedily.

"My god that was hard work" I panted as I handed the water back to Uar.

"Right, we're here… what now?" Tunnan asked. Brea elbowed him in the stomach.

Tunnan ended up coming on the journey. I'm not sure what's going on with him or what Uar and him talked about the night before we left, but he was here none-the-less and we needed the extra muscle to help us defeat Bres and his army. I tried not to dwell on it.

"I don't really know, I suppose I should have a look around and see if there's anything that might help me." I looked around very unsure of myself. The only thing on this rock apart from the grass I was sitting on was a little tree. I stood up and slowly walked over it.

"It's an oak sapling" Uar said as he gently put his hand on its branches. "The same type of tree that surrounds mother."

Zeg jumped on it and pulled out his sword. I smiled at him.

"This is a sign, I know it. This is significant." I said softly to Uar. Everyone was catching their breaths and not paying us too much attention or they were just letting us get on with it without an audience. Either way I was happy for it.

One of the leaves started to glow slightly under Uar's touch. Zeg jumped onto another branch afraid the glow would reach him. We all looked in awe as the bright glow filled the veins of the leave, then as soon as it happened it disappeared. Uar and I looked at each other and smiled. I leaned out and touched the tree. I could feel the glow run down my arm as it hit the little tree. Glowing letters formed on the trunk I kept my hand on the tree as the letters swirled around each other. I dared not look away in case something happened and they stopped. I didn't know if it was just me that could see them or if everyone could see it. I knew Uar could though, he put his hand on top of mine and the letters started to form a sentence.

Trust the light

"Trust the light" I whispered. "Trust the light" I said again a little louder. The letters slowly disappeared over the ocean in a straight line towards the cliff of the sacred lady. "Follow the light."

"We need to follow the light" I said to Uar.

I went to take a step over the edge where the letters had disappeared over the ocean. "What are you doing?" Uar yelled. "You're going to fall!" He pulled me back and hugged me.

I breathed him in and took a deep breath. "We need to trust the light, which means follow it and we need to follow it over to the cliff."

"Are you crazy? There's nothing there, you're going to fall to your death."

"Can you not see it?"

"See what?"

"The light." I could see a bridge of light following the letters' path to the top of the cliff. Everyone looked at me dumbfounded. "Look" I said as I grabbed some grass and threw it out in front of me.

Uar stared at the blades of grass that were sitting in mid-air. "Brigid, you've found the way"

I felt Zeg's tiny weight on my shoulder. He was ready to go, as was I.

"Yes, with your help Uar. Follow me. Follow exactly where I place my feet." I felt very important all of a sudden. They were all following and listening to what I said. I hoped I looked as cool as I felt at that moment.

I took a step forward into what would appear to be nothing. I could see the light, it was easy for me. I could see an invisible bridge about a metre wide stretching from Grisbid Rock to the cliff. The glow was faint but I could see it but nobody else could, not even Uar. Uar followed closely behind me, being careful to step where I had stepped. I took my first step slowly, just in case it was a trick, but I knew deep in my heart that it wasn't. Only myself and Uar could have done this, it needed both of us to unlock the access to the back of the cliff. That was why no one had found it before. I kept walking, one foot in front of the other. The wind was blowing strong, but not strong enough to knock us down. I ignored it and kept walking forward. Everyone was quiet as we walked in mid-air above the dark depths of Black's Bay. I had a creepy feeling something was watching us from its depths below, there was something there, not willing to show itself yet but I could feel it and I was certain it was not my mind playing tricks on me. This was not like the pretend monsters in my wardrobe. I prayed that we would make it to the end. It was a weird feeling. The ground under us was solid, it was a bridge, yet it was nothing. I tried not to think about it too hard and just get to the end. This was nearly over. Once we got over and entered the oak trees that guarded the horizon of the cliff, we would have done it. The Fomorians couldn't get in then, they wouldn't be able to pass.

CHAPTER 22

We finally got to the end with everyone accounted for. There were no nasty surprises as we crossed. It felt too easy. I held my hand out the entire way ready to burst out a fiery arrow if needed. Zeg had his little sword out ready to strike should the occasion need it. I had to calm him down at some points crossing the bridge as all I could see out the corner of my eye distracting me was a little sword waving frantically within my peripheral vision. I'd definitely give him five stars for dedication and determination. He was my little loyal warrior. I stepped gently onto the dirt and breathed a sigh of relief when everything seemed normal. I could feel the sun on my back and I could hear the rustling of the wind hitting the trees around me. Everyone stopped behind me, waiting and watching, anticipating my next move. What now? Tall oak trees flanked me on all sides. I could hear them calling out for me, I could hear her calling me, urging me to move forward, letting me know she was close. Zeg's energy increased, could he feel her too? My whole body was zinging with light and energy, my arm and hand glowed brightly showing the familiar patterns circling my hand and my arm. I took a step forward and came across no obstacles. No bolt of lightning burned me, the earth did not open and suck me underneath, which I half expected it to do. There were no bones of judgements singing to me, no force field stopping my advance, I was through, I was here, where I was supposed to be. This was what my existence was about, was me making it here, to this spot in this dimension. I turned and smiled and motioned for everyone to keep moving forward, it was safe. I moved aside so they could get through. We still needed to keep our voices down. The Fomorians were on the other side of these woods.

I looked at Brea and she had a tear on her cheek. She quickly wiped it away when she realised I'd seen it. She nodded her thanks to me in silence. I nodded back, but I didn't want to give anyone false hope, we hadn't won yet. Brigid was still frozen. I saw Tunnan out the corner of my eye take to the trees, watching guard with his bow and arrow. I smiled as he disappeared. It was a nice feeling knowing there was a secret assassin in the trees ready to shoot down any enemies.

Uar picked me up and spun me around with excitement. "Let's free mother."

"Yes, let's." I couldn't wait to meet her. To say I wasn't nervous was a lie, his mother was a goddess, the lady of the sacred flame, basically the meaning of life. What was I going to say to her?

We walked through the trees. There was no pathway to the middle of the woods as we weaved our way between tall oak trees, but I could feel her. I could feel her aura and her light. I nearly ran as I saw the clearing and Brigid. Tears streamed down my face as I bolted towards the statue. She looked astonishingly beautiful even frozen in stone. Her hands were up in the air and her head turned up towards the sky. Her long hair stood frozen in a fan around head, you could see the sadness and betrayal on her face when she'd realised that her family and friends had betrayed her and condemned her to death. Her long dress had frozen mid-air and it flew elegantly behind her, never meeting the ground again since that dreadful day.

Zeg was already there, teleporting to her side before we got there. He sat at her feet with his bum crack showing as he leant over and held on tightly to one of her toes. I came to his side and cried. "We're here, I'm here now. It will be alright." I placed my hand on her foot of stone.

I felt Uar beside me, I didn't need to look up to know it was him, I just knew.

"Mother, we are here, Brigid is here with your light. You are saved." He whispered as he kissed her stony foot. He kept kneeling and reached out with both of his hands. He turned and smiled at me. He nodded towards her other foot. I followed his lead and touched it with both hands. A sudden pulse burst through my body. Uar started chanting and our bodies started to light up. I could feel the familiar tingle engulf my body, it as electrifying. Our light surged into Brigid's feet gently cracking the stone as it went past. He kept chanting and I held on for dear life. It was starting to burn me, but I never let go. The cracking continued up her body, nothing fell, just covered her statue in hundreds of hair-line fractures, all the way up to the tips of her hair. The burning stopped and I turned to Uar. Our light had gone out. Had we failed? She was still frozen, had it not worked? I started to freak out.

"Uar?" I asked questioningly. Wondering whether we weren't enough to free her from her stony prison. Had she been frozen too long, were we too late.

He smiled as he stood up. He took my hand and turned it over so the fire arrow mark on my palm was facing upwards. "It's your turn now."

He didn't need to explain, I knew. I took a couple of steps back and aimed my hand towards his mother and took the shot with my fire arrow. The stone exploded around us and I ducked as small debris flew past me. I heard a thud and saw a figure fall to the ground.

I gasped "Brigid!"

Uar ran towards her and picked her near lifeless body up "Mother!"

She looked up at her son with her vivid green eyes in recognition. "Uar my son."

Her voice was so faint, so beautiful it echoed like when she used to talk to me. I kept my distance letting Uar gently pick her up and sit her down on a large rock. She kept touching his face and kissing his cheeks. Tears were streaming down her face. "Oh Uar my boy, you did not abandon me."

"No mother, I would never."

"Luchar?"

Uar shook his head. She understood. Her middle son had not helped, but I had a feeling she already knew this.

Zeg jumped on her shoulder "Oh Zeg, my dear friend." Was all she said as Zeg kissed and hugged her neck. Zeg had tears streaming down his little brownie cheeks.

She looked up at me and I stood completely still, inwardly freaking out. She was looking at me. The goddess was looking at me. "Thank you Brigid" she simply said as she smiled a maternal smile at me and bowed her head.

I smiled back feeling her warmth. "You are more than welcome your goddess, um Brigid, my lady" I was all flabbergasted, I didn't know what to call her.

She laughed weakly at my efforts. Uar hung onto her as she sat down. She was very weak, but she was alive. She was beautiful just as I pictured her to be. Her white gown flowed around her and her glowing orange hair fell down her back. Her vivid green eyes shone out over her delicate pointy features.

Slowly Brea came up to her and knelt down in front of her. "Mother" she whispered.

Brigid put her hand on top of Brea's head. "My child, thank you." Brea nodded and stood up and walked back as the next one came up. Once everyone had greeted their goddess and Brigid had regained enough strength to walk we decided we had to go.

"Is she okay?" I whispered to the closest person to me, which happened to be Yute. I silently cringed, waiting for the snide remark.

He grunted at me before he answered but was surprisingly civil. "She's weak she needs water and sun to rejuvenate her." I could feel he was warming up to me, but still held some reservations, he must have trust issues, maybe daddy issues. I did save his life after all, was that not enough to gain his trust. "We'll take her to the well, that will help her."

I nodded. Right, she needed the water from the well in the middle of town. We could do that. We might meet some resistance if we bang into any Fomorians on the way, but we could do that I was sure. She needed to get her strength back so she could defeat her husband and have her revenge and bring back the life to the Otherworld and save her people.

I led them back to the invisible bridge again. The front of the woods and the bones of judgement were blocked with Bres' army, this was the only way out and we were the only ones that could cross. Uar and Hagrid helped Brigid walk through the trees. She was still incredibly weak so Hagrid picked her up and carried her to quicken the pace. She'd been frozen in stone for hundreds and hundreds of years, I was surprised she was even talking.

The wind suddenly slowed down, the air thickened as anxiety surrounded me like a blanket. Something was wrong. Uar also felt it and moved closer to his mother.

"BRIGID!"

I dropped to my knees as the powerful sonic boom ran through my body, Zeg's weight left my shoulder as I fell. I knew that voice. Bres was here. The sting ran up my thighs as the impact of the ground vibrated upwards from my knees. Memories of my prison fuelled my fear of what was to come.

Zeg teleported with his little sword directed at Bres's left eye. Bres brushed Zeg aside like a piece of trash. I saw Zeg's little body fly over the trees with the power of Bres's force.

"No!" I screamed.

I looked up with tears welling up in my eyes. Bres' huge powerful frame stood in front of the invisible bridge. Everyone froze. Cichol was beside him, emotionless. He wouldn't look at me. There was a whole army behind them, lined up along the horizon of the cliff and down the bridge with their grotesque forms and red capes snapping with the wind. We were trapped, there was no way out. He must've followed us.

"My WIFE! How happy I am to see you." He boomed between clenched teeth. He relaxed and smiled when he saw how weak she was. "What? You're not happy to see me... why that doesn't seem very fair... because I have certainly missed YOU!" The last word he shouted as spittle sprayed out in front of him. I could see his body grow bigger with this anger.

"Bres" I heard the goddess weakly whisper reaching out to him.

"And my son, how good to see you again. Betrayal looks good on you" Bres spat.

Uar tensed. Everyone was at a standstill. No one wanted to move, frightened to start something that they may not be able to finish.

"Father" he hissed between clenched teeth. Uar nodded in acknowledgement towards his father.

"Oh and look who we have here." Bres' power pulled me up off my knees and held me in mid-air. An invisible force held me up and left my feet dangling. "It's my little pet. Where did you go? I had such great plans for you but I must thank you for showing me another way to my wife." He smirked evilly to me.

I could feel Uar move closer to me as he felt his father's threat towards me.

"Yeah, how did those plans work out for you?" I replied with sarcasm dripping from my mouth. I was not going to show fear. He did not control me. I turned my palm up and shot out a fire arrow aimed at his head.

He blasted it aside with a swipe of his hand. "Ha, is that…"

"Now!" Uar shouted.

An arrow sliced across Bres's cheek, blood appeared as his roar filled the woods.

I fell to the ground as Bres released me with the shock of the attack. Tunnan must've fired the arrow from the trees.

All hell broke loose. The Fomorian's moved forward, as did the Gold Belts. Tunnan's arrows started shadowing the sun as they came flying down from the trees.

The first Fomorian took a fire arrow to the stomach as he advanced on me. I could sense the goddess to the side of me. Uar was with her, but he was torn. Should he be protecting his mother or me.

"Protect her!" I yelled out. "I'm fine! I'll be okay, protect her!"

He nodded as I turned and punched a Fomorian in the face and ran my sword up through his neck. The stink of his blood was rancid. I didn't have time to vomit before the next assault came at me. I was knocked to the ground as Brea and a Fomorian fell on top of me. I heard the strangled scream as I stuck my knife through the side of the Fomorian.

"Thanks" Brea breathed as she jumped up to push another one off us.

The weight of the dead Fomorian was immense. I pushed and tried to roll him off me, but I couldn't get him off. I knew I had more strength than this. I drew on my light and pushed him forward, he flew through the air as strength filled my body. I was literally glowing. A switch had gone off like in training at Aberline Castle. I could anticipate what was about to happen, I was lethal, I was unstoppable. I blocked out what was happening around me except for my assailants coming for me. I knew Uar would have his Mother, she'd be safe, but out of the corner of my eye I could see her suddenly disappear. Where did she go? Hagrid was close behind and realisation hit. He must be cloaking her to hide her from the battle - wise move. I knifed a Fomorian in the skull as it went for a kill blow on one of our own. I didn't have time to check to see who it was before I was lifted off the ground and found my legs dangling in the air. Bres had me again, I couldn't move. He turned my body to face him and lifted me high above everyone else. Gravity pulled against his power, pulling my body apart. The smile on his face was pure evil. He meant to kill me this time, I doubted I was going to get out of this alive. He dragged me forward towards him through the air near the back of the cliff where he had retreated away from the battle. Coward I thought to myself. I could see everyone fighting below me as I floated past. A Fomorian dropped to the ground as Uar chopped off his head and two more Fomorian quickly took his place. Blood squirted all over him. Why wasn't he with his mother? I could see Uar look at me quickly, fear drained his face as he saw me floating towards his father. He ran forward, bowling whatever was in his way.

"Brigid!" He yelled.

Bres laughed as he dropped me on the ground in front of him. I crumpled like a sack of potatoes. Cichol stood with him, emotionless, refusing to look at me. Was he still with me?

I turned to look at Bres.

"You should not be alive" he spat.

I was pushed to the side as Uar jumped over the top of me and Cichol dove in front of Bres.

"No!" They both screamed.

They both fell to the ground as Bres lowered his bow back down to his side.

"No!" I screamed, I crawled to Uar. He looked up at me as I grabbed him and shook his head looking ahead of him to Cichol. I followed his stare "Hayden?" I whispered. "Hayden!" I screamed as I ran towards him. He was down and he wasn't getting up. Blood pooled on the ground beside him as I saw the huge arrow sticking out from his chest. "What have you done?!" I screamed at Bres. "What have you done?!" I kept screaming. I scooped Hayden up in my arms and kissed his forehead as I rocked him. His eyes stayed closed. He was lifeless. "No, no, no" I kept chanting. I didn't want to believe that he was dead, he couldn't be dead. Not my Hayden, he was my best friend. Tears rolled down my face and my body convulsed with sadness. "Don't leave me" I whispered against his cheek.

Bres shook his head. "Why would he do that?" he whispered looking confused. "Why?" He looked at me with pure fury. "He hated you! Why would he DO THAT!" His words got louder until he shouted the last few words.

His shouting was stopped by soft hands touching his face. Bres turned quickly to the owner. It was Brigid, the goddess. She was standing beside him by the edge of the cliff, her white dress blowing in the wind behind her. It looked like a scene from a movie.

She kept her hands on his face looking up at him tenderly. "I forgive you" she whispered.

"What?" Bres tried to pull away but Brigid held him tight not letting him go. She was still powerful even if she wasn't running on all of her cylinders.

"I forgive you." She simply said again.

Bres's face contorted as Brigid pulled him closer towards her. He reached for his bow but Brigid pushed it away, he reached for his knife but Brigid dissolved it into crumbs. "This isn't fair. You, you were not supposed to win, you betrayed me" he whispered. He was starting to relax under her touch.

Brigid shushed him.

Bres's massive fist burst through Brigid's power and stopped just before it met its mark. Brigid simply smiled and caressed his arm gently forcing it behind his back out of harms reach.

"I forgive you" she repeated.

Bres's face softened as Brigid pulled him gently towards her to kiss him. He wrapped his arms around her. "My little one" he breathed as he kissed her back. They were the only two people in the world at this moment of time. There was love there once, it was clear to see. Somewhere it had gotten twisted and spoiled along the way. Brigid wrapped one of her arms around his enormous back as she deepened the kiss. Her other hand continued to stroke the side of his face. I couldn't believe what I was seeing. They were supposed to hate each other.

A soft glow started to engulf them. "No" Bres whispered. "What are you doing? No." He tried to pull back as stone ran up the length of their bodies but it was too late. The goddess had tricked him. Brigid held on tight as the stone encased them both and froze them where they stood, holding each other like lovers. Then there was silence. Nothing – not even the wind blew. We all looked at the goddess and her god embraced like lovers forever in stone overlooking Black's Bay. I held onto Hayden, wondering what the hell was going on.

A sudden pain ran through my back, something was crawling up my back. "Get it off!" I screamed as I pulled away from Hayden. "Somethings in there, get it off!" I ripped my chest armour off to try and ease the burn.

In the distance I could hear Uar roaring too as he ripped off his chest armour.

Brea stopped me before I could rip off my top. "Are you okay?" She asked. Her face was muddy and bloody. One of her eyes had closed over.

"My back, something was crawling up my back." I pulled my top down. "It's stopped now though." I felt a bit foolish as everyone starred at me.

Uar ran and hugged me tightly. He'd pulled his chest armour and cape off, I could feel the warmth of his skin and his tight muscles against me. I relaxed in his grip. "Hayden" I whispered as I looked over at his still body. The pool of dark red blood was larger now.

He ran his hand through my hair to comfort me. "I know, I'm sorry Brigid."

I looked over to Hayden lying on the ground. I knew he was dead. He hadn't moved. My best friend was gone.

Cichol and Uar had both tried to safe me. They both jumped in the way of Bres' enormous arrow that was supposed to kill me and would have killed me if Cichol hadn't taken the hit. He'd stayed true to his word. He protected me to the very end. I choked up again and I hid my head in Uar's chest, not wanting the others to see me cry.

The Fomorians were pulling back, one of them grabbed Hayden by the legs and started dragging him across the ground, retreating to safety. I made a move towards Hayden but Uar pushed me back to him. "He's with his people Brigid."

I cried. He was right. But I was his people too. I nodded letting him know I understood.

Without their leader the Fomorians looked lost. They needed to regroup. I was glad for it. My body and soul had been ripped apart already and I didn't think I had anything left in me.

There should have been lots of cheering going on, the fight was over, we'd won, the sun was shining, life would grow again in the Otherworld and the Fomorians were retreating – but there wasn't.

Their Mother was gone again, she'd barely walked half a kilometre before she was encased back in her stony tomb again overlooking the ocean. She'd made a huge sacrifice for her people trapping Bres with her. She must've thought this was the only way. Why else would she do it.

Uar walked over to his Mother and hugged her. He talked to her, I didn't know what he said I couldn't hear him but I could see his back.

"Uar, my god what is on your back?" I walked over and ran my hands over it. "It looks some sort of tattoo." He turned to stare at me. "It's true, your back is covered with black writing." I looked closer. I had no idea what it said, it just looked like a bunch of scribble and symbols to me. "How weird."

"Turn around, let me see yours." He said.

"What?"

"Turn around, your back was burning to?" He was right my back felt like something was crawling up it as it ate through my skin.

I turned around and pulled the back of my top up. He laughed. "Mother."

"What do you mean mother? Do I have it on my back too?"

"Yes we both do."

It all started to sink in. "This must've something to do with what your Mother told me."

"She told you something? When?"

"When she was kissing your Dad" I cringed at the thought of the memory, yuck – why would anyone want to kiss him, he was such an ass. "I could hear her in my mind. She told me that we needed to find the sapience. Both you and I had to find it together. She was very adamant on that." I turned to Uar. "But I have no idea what that means, do you?"

"I may have an idea" He said glumly as he kept investigating my back.

"Uar what is it, what does it mean?"

"It means this isn't over yet."

The story of Brigid continues and is currently being written… keep your eye out.

DID YOU ENJOY THIS BOOK? It would be awesome if you leave a review on the site you purchased it from. Every review makes a difference.

ALSO BY NEISHA NILSEN
SACRIFICE - The Protector Saga #1
INCLUSION - The Protector Saga #2